THE TURNED GODS SERIES
CHARACTER COMPANION

GALIN'S ALLEY

JOYCE SERRANO

INTRODUCTION

Prequel to Original Grace in The Turned Gods Series timeline. The story of Galin and Vivienne takes place in 1901, Italy.

CHAPTER ONE

Galin wasn't happy about the time it was taking to get to the ship. Driving a four-horse wagon filled with wine crates through tight, heavily crowded streets took patience. It was the one thing he lacked today. He usually enjoyed the atmosphere of the city. But this morning he was on a tight schedule. Another one wouldn't be coming until next week if he missed the cargo ship today. Staying another week wasn't an issue for him since he planned on returning on the next train. The main problem was he had nowhere to store the wine for that long.

Genova was the largest port in Europe in 1901. It was also the main exodus point going to America. Most traveling through were of low means who could barely scrape together enough to book passage in steerage. Space was at a premium in the city and there wasn't an infrastructure to support the droves of people pouring through needing accommodation. Galin was fortunate not to be in that position. His family had means to afford the finest accommodations. Places he had access to always had rooms available.

The streets erupted in a burst of anger as a loud motor wagon made its way through the constricted street crossing in front of Galin's rig. Motorized vehicles had only recently begun dotting the city's landscape. Reception of this new technology was not warm. Along with it came a pressing speed to the slower pace of a society used to steam trains and horses.

Galin was snapped out of his wandering thoughts. Someone had stumbled into one of the horses, causing him to push into his yoke mate. The mare shifted over into a stream of people, knocking over a woman. Galin was off the wagon into the street before she had hit the ground. He pulled her up from behind, stopping the mare from trampling over her. Once she had her balance, she spun around. Upon seeing Galin had been the driver, the woman unleashed a stream of forceful Italian, far too quickly for Galin to understand, though her vibrant tone made it easy enough to discern her intentions.

The woman was tall and slender without being too thin. Her lips were full and naturally rosy. She had dark, black hair and deep, brown eyes that appeared nearly black as well, until a streak of errant morning sunlight hit them. Like most of the native population, her skin was smooth, olive, and tanned. She was very pretty, probably under forty by his assessment. Galin imagined she could be striking with a little more attention to her appearance.

Her clothing reflected the rest of the working class - a simple ankle length shift dress and apron with a fish basket in hand. From her scent, she worked in the market, likely as a fishmonger or possibly a cook. Galin was more inclined to believe the former. Her hands were clean and calloused in the places they would be from years of knife work. The apron she wore appeared clean, although it had been stained yellow in the places she would use to wipe her hands. And then there was the blood. No matter how clean it looked, to Galin, it would always smell of blood.

He fumbled through some rudimentary Italian, choosing his words carefully. "My apologies, ma'am. My horse was bumped. Are you injured?"

She keyed into his glaring lack of vocabulary, slowing her speech, but not her volume, to reply. "You can't drive them through these crowds! You should be walking them, so you don't kill anyone!"

She straightened herself, wiped her apron aggressively, then spun on her heel and disappeared into the crowd. Galin stared awkwardly in the direction she had gone until he had lost sense of her. He slowly took up the mare's bridle, guiding the team through the sea of travelers.

By the time Galin drew up to the dock, Lukkas had already offloaded his cargo onto the ship. He was standing with the loadmaster, reviewing the manifest and stalling.

"It's about time. You nearly missed it." Lukkas slapped Galin on the back, speaking to his brother in Danish.

The dockworkers seized on the cart quickly, hauling the precious cargo onto the ship. This was an important shipment for the brothers. Before today, they had only distributed locally. A procurement manager from one of the biggest hotels in New York had sent them a telegram. The owner, having visited Genova, had taken a liking to one of their reds and placed an order for two hundred bottles. If it sold, the winery would have opportunities to distribute to the entire hotel chain. This transaction needed to go well since they had only recently purchased the winery. Expanding their market throughout Europe had been their primary goal.

Getting into the American market, however, was something they hadn't imagined possible.

Galin was relieved to have gotten to the ship before it pulled out. In Danish, he said to Lukkas, "Sorry. I nearly killed a woman in the streets."

Lukkas flashed an overly animated, concerned expression. "I told you! You should have fed before you left."

Galin scoffed and spoke in an elevated whisper. "Lukkas! The horse nearly trampled her in the street. I didn't bite her."

Lukkas let out a hearty laugh. "You should have seen the look on your face. You are far too serious, Galin. I was joking."

"You shouldn't joke like that, Lukkas. You have no idea who might understand what you're saying." Galin admonished his younger brother.

"Galin, look around you. No one is paying any attention to us. They're all occupied with their own thoughts of getting away from here." Lukkas gestured around the docks.

"You should still be more careful with your speech in public," Galin rebuked. He remembered very clearly the dark times when human fear had nearly driven them into extinction. Lukkas was too young to remember, but Galin couldn't forget the horrifying scene of their mother's beheading. The brothers were fortunately spared their parents' fate, being mistaken for humans. They escaped with the few remaining members of their clan into safety and centuries in isolation. Their people had finally come together with all other known clans, becoming a single worldwide community. Gaining a foothold in legitimate business and politics was key to ensuring their safety. It was a delicate time for all of them.

Lukkas was much more relaxed about the attentiveness of humanity. Most were sheep, droning through their lives, oblivious to what was going on around them. Belief in magic and monsters had waned through the ages. Even if they had gone into the middle of the square and announced they were vampires, no one would believe them. They weren't the grotesque creatures confined to darkness that fairy tales said they should be. The days of excessive indulgence in debauchery had come to an end with the extermination. Survival dictated they evolve. In only a few hundred years, they had become more humane than humans. They didn't have untenable blood thirst or go on insatiable, murderous rampages. No one could conceive these modern, sophisticated men were the monsters of old, nightmarish stories created to scare children into submission.

Galin, on the other hand, understood exactly what mortal fear could do. Lukkas wasn't yet born when humans began hunting them. They were covert, isolating and picking them off one at a time. Galin saw the resulting torture that wiped out entire clans. He found the beheaded and burned bodies. He saw the missing teeth and extremities. He saw the lengths terrified humans would go to. It was something he was unwilling to face again.

Lukkas saw the apprehension on his brother's face. "You're right, Galin. I will be more aware of my company when speaking."

With the wagon empty, the brothers unstrapped two of the horses for their personal transportation and paid to have the carts driven back to the vineyard. Their business in Genova wasn't finished yet. A few members of the Board leadership were here to meet with them in four days' time. Until then, they would enjoy themselves.

The streets were far less crowded once the cargo and passenger ships pulled out of port. Traveling on horseback was a much easier way to traverse the city as they made their way to the most luxurious hotel available, the Grand Hotel Savoia. Upon the brothers' arrival, their horses were taken to board. They entered and approached the lobby desk. The opulence rendered Lukkas speechless. His mouth hung agape. The ceilings were as high as any he had seen. And there was a small symphony of musicians playing in the far corner. Galin, not wanting to appear outside his element, held his astonishment in as they approached the desk.

Galin prepared his best Italian. "Galin and Lukkas Eliassen to check in, please."

The gentleman at the desk recognized Galin's obvious discomfort with the language and spoke in English. "We accommodate English, French, and German languages. Would one of those be your preferred?"

Since the gentleman at the desk had spoken English, Galin chose to respond in kind. "You are too kind, sir. I am much more fluent in English." The conversation would continue in the chosen language.

"Mrs. Eliassen has already checked into your suite of rooms." The clerk nodded toward Lukkas. "She was picked up from the nine-thirty train along with your baggage. Here are your keys." He handed them each a key of their own. "Will you be requiring anything else?"

"Yes. Would you please send up a fresh tray of coffee?" Galin asked.

"Certainly, sir." The clerk snapped at a bellhop. "Show the gentlemen to their suite."

Galin and Lukkas followed the bellhop to their rooms, where Grace was waiting in the main living space. She was lounging on a chaise in front of the wide window with her head buried in a book. It was a usual position for her. The woman read anything she was able to set her hands on. Lukkas studied her for a moment. Her long hair swept up in a dolmen style worn by sophisticated women of that time. It was preferred so as not to muss under an ornate, wide-brimmed hat when they were out walking. She was still wearing her traveling suit minus the jacket, hat, and boots.

The sun shone across her face, highlighting a few unruly, dark tendrils twisting down one cheek and landing on her chest. Grace was a slightly above average looking woman. Not someone likely to be remembered in a crowd with the exception of her large, clear, deep green eyes. When she smiled, they lit as if the sun were inside of them. People were drawn to her in an inexplicable way. The sheer joy of life seeped from her every pore. She was empathetic and peaceful, but wasn't a vampire like they were. No one knew what she was, other than an immortal. She appeared to be in her early to mid-thirties. At this point, she and Lukkas had been together for over six hundred years. Before that, she had a thousand she could remember.

Lukkas frowned at her unsophisticated position on the chaise. She laid across, propped by pillows with her bare feet draped over one of the arms, with her skirt pooled up onto her thighs. She looked up from her book, smiling widely, when she noticed the men enter the room.

Lukkas was of average height and fit with medium blond hair. He looked to be in his late thirties, mostly due to the age that styling of this period added to one's appearance. He currently had a mustache that Grace did not care for. She thought if a man were to go as far as growing a mustache; he needed full facial hair to balance it out like Galin had. But Lukkas liked it, so she held her opinion to herself. The trend would change in a few years, anyway. It always did.

Galin was slightly taller than Lukkas, a little heavier and more muscular than his younger sibling. Depending on the amount of facial hair he was sporting, he looked to be somewhere in late thirties to early forties. He had thick, light brown hair that carried some reddish tones, especially through his beard. Both men had blue eyes, but Galin's were brighter than Lukkas's. Even without facial hair, he appeared much older than Lukkas; likely because of the hardship he had endured raising his orphaned infant sibling.

"You're back." Grace was glad to see them. "Business done?"

"For now." Lukkas walked over, sitting on the edge of the chaise. "What trouble have you been up to?"

"None. I came straight here from the train. The better question is, what trouble am I planning to get up to?" Grace's smile hadn't faded as she closed her book, carefully marking her place with a satin ribbon.

Lukkas placed his hand on her arm, smiling back at her. "I know better than to ask that particular question."

"Lukkas, I've been sitting for hours. Can't we go exploring in the city?"

"We've been riding nearly all night. Personally, I would appreciate a bath and a nap," Lukkas answered. He wasn't used to physical endeavors as much as his brother was. He preferred dealing with the more cordial elements of the business. His skills were best suited for finance and contracts.

Grace wasn't pleased with being stuck inside. "Then I'll go on my own."

"No. It is not appropriate for you to be without an escort in the city. Things are different here." Appearances were extremely important to Lukkas. They needed to stay within the confines of proper society.

"Then I'll have the concierge find me a guide." Her face turned stern. Grace wasn't one to be told what she could and couldn't do, especially by a man.

Galin, always the diplomat, felt it time to intervene. "No need for that, Grace. I would be happy to escort you." He also had an ulterior motive. He wanted to find the woman from the street. She had been on his mind since their encounter earlier that morning. There was something about the way she had carried herself. She was proud, confident, and fearless. Those were refreshing traits for women these days, especially within the social circles they recently found themselves in. Most women were eager to please men of means. This woman didn't seem to care about anything outside the possibility that he had been irresponsible with his horses.

"Thank you, Galin. I would love to explore the city with you." Grace rose to her feet, smoothing her skirt.

Lukkas was thankful for the compromise. "Well, it seems to be settled then. I can nap and join you two for dinner later."

Grace was putting her shoes back on when Lukkas cleared his throat. She looked up sideways.

"What?"

"You're not going out in your traveling suit, are you?"

Grace rolled her eyes. "You know, I used to wear the same dress for weeks. Now I change four times a day. I'll be so happy when this ridiculous period is over." She stomped to her room to change into her walking skirt and blouse.

Galin smirked behind her. Lukkas smirked back at him. "You too," Lukkas said.

The smile slid off Galin's face. He pulled off his riding jacket and tossed it on a chair. Without acknowledging the comment, he headed to his own room to change into something clean.

CHAPTER TWO

Galin and Grace took a carriage down to the city center where they could stroll through the market. The ocean breeze was cool against the warm, early afternoon sun. The morning crowd had disbursed, leaving mostly tourists and casual towns people out strolling. They shopped outside stalls and businesses along their route. Grace always purchased small toys and books for the children of whatever village they lived in. She couldn't resist seeing their smiling faces when presented with the tiniest of treasures. At the rate she was going, she could accumulate a small horde by the time they hired a staff for the vineyard.

When she went into a dress shop, Galin made his way across the street where several gentleman escorts were gathered. The shop tables outside were set up for serving coffee and aperitifs. Galin thought it was an excellent business choice - serve alcohol to men who had no other purpose than to stay in view of the dress shop while they waited. A roaming tobacconist made his way round presenting his wares. Galin purchased a pouch of cherry bourbon leaf for his pipe and carried on pleasant conversations with various gentlemen as they came and went. As he waited, he scanned the market stalls as far as he could see for the woman. Her scent told him which direction she was, even how far away she was. She had, to the current point, eluded his sight.

It was nearly an hour before Grace emerged from the dress shop. She was smiling, graciously thanking the shop attendant, but Galin could tell she was irritated. He bid adieu to his fellow purposeless acquaintances and crossed the street to meet her. Offering his arm to Grace, who accepted it elegantly, they walked out of range where she could voice her irritation.

"I so detest being ogled and pawed in that manner. You would think these women had never seen a tattoo before!"

Galin stifled a snicker. "Grace, you have twenty-three."

She then burst out in laughter. He couldn't help but join her. She was pleasantly infectious.

"What can I say? I am a Viking. I only wish I knew where some of them had come from." Her smile changed from happy to wistful.

He patted her hand sympathetically. "Not to worry Grace. We'll find your story one day. And I'm certain it will be epic."

She hugged his arm. "It doesn't matter now. Knowing my past won't change where I am. I'm grateful to have you and Lukkas."

While they walked, Galin could smell the scent of the woman getting stronger. He thought he was being covert, searching the crowd. Unfortunately for him, Grace's observation was nearly as keen.

"Galin, what are you looking for?" She had drawn him to a halt in the middle of the street.

It was of no use deflecting the question. She would know. "The woman from this morning. The one I told you about in the carriage, that I nearly trampled."

"Ahhhh." Grace taunted him amusedly.

"I wanted to make certain she was uninjured," Galin retorted, attempting to appear innocent.

"Uh-huh. I'm sure." Seeing he had taken an interest in the woman, she continued to tease him.

Galin sighed, defeated at the teasing. "Let's just go back to the hotel, then."

"No. If you don't find her today, you'll never have the courage. Let's go." She nudged him forward.

He had no choice in the matter now. Once Grace had something in her head, it was as good as done. They walked a few blocks further. The scent was strong. He turned, catching sight of her.

"Now don't be conspicuous. She's in the fish stand on the right. The one with the blue banner." Galin was actually nervous.

Grace nonchalantly scanned the booths up and down the right side of the street. "Now I see what caught your interest. She's lovely."

"Grace, this isn't a good idea. Let's go back."

"Too late." She attempted to pull her hand away from his arm, but only as a courtesy. He held onto her and hoped she wouldn't make a spectacle of him in public. She snickered lightly, holding a bag up in front of them. She made her arm less solid, sliding it out through his.

"Sometimes I really wish you couldn't do that." Galin wasn't shocked, although he had hoped she wouldn't have used her phasing ability in such a large crowd.

"No one saw," she replied, grinning.

Grace approached the woman at the fish booth. Galin had a choice; follow her or stand in the middle of the street, clearly looking like an idiot. He chose to follow, lagging a few steps behind. The woman smiled at Grace. It quickly faded when she saw Galin come up to her side. Thinking neither had a grasp of Italian, she placed a broad smile back on her face.

Her language sounded overly sweet to Galin's ears. "How lovely, the imbecile from the port this morning. What can I do for you?"

Grace let out a hearty laugh. The woman's face appeared mortified, although her posture had not waned. "My apologies Signora. I did not mean to insult your husband."

Grace replied in perfect Italian. "Never apologize when you're right. And he's not my husband; he's my brother-in-law. I'm Grace. And you are?" She removed her glove, holding out her hand to the woman.

The woman bit her lower lip. "Signora, no. My hands are filthy."

Grace gave her a stern but somehow friendly look, inching her hand farther forward. The woman wiped her hands as best she could before grasping Grace's timidly. Grace gripped it firmly, covering it with her other gloved hand.

"Never be ashamed of being someone who works hard." Grace stared intently into the woman's deep, dark eyes. "Your name?"

"Vivienne." She nodded her head, smiling authentically this time.

"Well Vivienne, may I introduce you to Galin? He was concerned his horse had injured you this morning." Grace released Vivienne's hand, nudging Galin forward.

Galin hadn't understood much of the conversation. He did realize this was an introduction. He stepped closer, grasping

Vivienne's hand. He gently kissed the back of it, drawing her scent in deeply. Vivienne appeared embarrassed and pulled her hand away quickly, flashing a nervous smile.

"Do you speak another language? German or French maybe?" Grace asked Vivienne.

"Je parle français," Vivienne replied. Galin was relieved. He had an excellent command of the French language.

Galin smiled warmly at Vivienne, continuing their conversation in French. "I would like to apologize for the events this morning. Please let me make it up to you. Would you join us for dinner?"

Vivienne shook her head nervously again. She was clearly embarrassed by her attire and her station, which was glaringly beneath theirs. She wouldn't be welcome in the places they would go.

"No, I couldn't."

Grace was having none of it. She had an idea. "Oh, and we were so hoping to have a guide to take us to somewhere the locals go. Not the stuffy, overpriced places we usually end up eating at when we're here. I so hate wearing these clothes. When I'm home at the winery," Grace leaned forward, whispering, "I wear trousers."

Galin's hearing was incredibly acute being a vampire. He attempted to conceal a snicker. Grace and Vivienne did not conceal theirs. Vivienne was decidedly more comfortable with that suggestion.

"If you're sure. Some of these places can be rough," Vivienne replied.

"Oh, I think we can handle it," Galin smirked.

"I drop off the money from the stand after I close. Meet me at eight at this address." Vivienne scrawled an address on a piece of butcher paper and handed it to Galin. She looked at the pair suspiciously.

He took the paper. He and Grace left the stand in the direction of the hotel.

"She doesn't think we're going to show up." Grace glanced sideways at Galin.

"Won't she be surprised when we do then?" He replied.

Back at the hotel, Galin was surprised when Lukkas agreed to go with them. He normally preferred finer dining situations, where he was able to establish business or political connections. Lukkas told Galin sometimes it was beneficial to have less dignified connections in your pocket. Opportunities could be found in the most curious places.

With the way they were dressed to meet their new friend, they would need to escape the hotel without being detected. An exit through the lobby or even kitchens was out of the question. It wasn't a difficult task. Their rooms were only on the fourth floor. None of the three would come to any harm by jumping from that height. The main full balcony was well lit. The balconet in Galin's room was on the dark side of the building. Leaving it open would let them easily back in again.

They moved through the streets quickly and quietly. Their speed made seeing them difficult for an average human, and the dark made it impossible. Lukkas kept hold of Grace's hand. Though she had the same speed as they did, she couldn't see as well in the dark. Galin and Lukkas had night vision reserved for predators. Her advantage lay in being able to phase through things in her path. There wasn't a need to see something if you had the ability to pass through it without being detected.

Their pace ended in a dark alley a few blocks from where they were to meet Vivienne. They would walk the last section at a normal, human speed. Galin was excited. He was intrigued by her acceptance of a stranger's invitation. To him, everything about her was intriguing. Maybe she had only accepted because Grace had been with him. Grace had a magnetic presence that drew others to her, made them trust her. He guessed he would never know. Not that it made a difference now.

They were early. Galin smelled her coming before she turned the corner. He was pleased when he saw her emerge from the alley. She had changed into a long straight skirt and loose white blouse similar to the one Grace had chosen to wear. The apron was gone, and her hands scrubbed free of blood. The fish scent had been replaced with light lavender. There was another scent that followed her. It was an earthy scent of dirt, soap, and sweat. Galin couldn't see around the corner of the alley. It was obvious to him she wasn't alone. A large, dark figure emerged from the side of the building.

"Ah, I'm pleasantly surprised you came. I hope you don't mind. I've brought my brother Vito. He doesn't believe it is safe for me walking the streets alone at night. It's nearly impossible for me to dissuade him." Vivienne extended her hand toward the massive man behind her.

"We weren't certain you would come," Galin said to Vivienne. He extended his hand toward Vito, locking his gaze. "Thank you for your escort, sir. I must agree dark streets are no place for a lady alone at night. We are grateful to have your company this evening. I am Galin and this is my brother, Lukkas, and his wife, Grace." Lukkas and Grace had been together for centuries and although they had never married, the aesthetics of the period demanded them to act as if they had.

Vito reached out, grasping Galin's hand. While Galin wasn't a small man, his hand was completely engulfed by Vito's thick, meaty one. He could feel the strength of Vito's grip. It was far stronger than that of an average human man, although it still paled in comparison to the strength of which Galin was capable.

"Thank you for the invitation. I had no intention of intruding. I only wanted to see her here safely."

Vito's French was difficult to understand through his thick Italian accent. The grammar was accurate, noting to Galin's ear of at least a primary education. From his speech, he seemed more intelligent than someone of his brawn was usually credited with. He released Galin's hand, taking Lukkas's next.

"It's no intrusion at all, sir. You are more than welcome to join us. We insist." Lukkas said, further extending the invitation.

Vito accepted. With the evening's company set, they walked a few blocks south parallel to the sea. They stopped in front of a building that looked more like an old traveler's house than a restaurant. It brought back fond memories of long forgotten adventures in a far-off land, to Galin's mind.

They entered and were directed to seats at the far end of a long table half-filled with others. It would be a family style dinner where you ate whatever the cook decided to serve. Galin insisted on paying the price for their group, stifling Vito's objection.

Evening meals across Europe were prolonged casual affairs, sometimes lasting hours. This place was no different. Courses beginning with bread and herbed olive oil were brought out to be shared at steady intervals. Service was well paced, allowing for lengthy conversations.

Galin, Vivienne, and Vito sat on one side of the table while Lukkas and Grace sat across from them. They discussed easy topics at first - the winery the brothers had recently purchased, city places of interest and food. Their excitement over their first wine shipment to the Americas took the space between the first and second courses.

Next, it was Vivienne and Vito's turn to recount their short history. Galin had been correct in assuming they were educated. They had been raised on a winery themselves. Their father had a large one handed down from his father. A series of poor business decisions paired with an infestation of Phylloxera wiped out the season's crop and forced the sale of their family's legacy before Vito and Vivienne had a chance to inherit it. But it wasn't before Vivienne's father had married her off to the man who caused their downfall. Once he had alleviated them of the majority of their assets, he left Vivienne and her family to their destitution. He had disappeared nearly twenty years ago, and she had never gotten over the betrayal. The loss was enhanced shortly after his departure when their father died, leaving the two of them, barely out of their teens, on their own.

Vito had finally landed himself a position in a bottling warehouse where he had worked for the last twelve years. Vivienne worked in several hotels and restaurants, only recently gaining employment at the fish stand. Hard work didn't bother her. The stand owner let her run things as she wished as long as she gave him half the profits each day. The man had a few stands in the market, so it was a good investment for him. Having a woman at his stand meant more male customers. It was a favorable situation for anyone to have, especially a woman who had few opportunities at that time.

The conversation was becoming a little more personal. The wine was enhancing Vivienne's urge to share her opinion, especially after Galin had made a remark about his first impression of her.

"I'm not saying that, Galin. What I am saying is, if you don't rely on others, you won't be disappointed by them."

"That's a little cynical, don't you think? Or is it an excuse to keep people out of your life?" Galin wouldn't normally have said something so rude to a woman he had only recently met. Vivienne was different from the other women he knew. There was no pretense with her.

"I don't keep people out of my life. I just don't rely on anyone to solve my problems for me. My choices and the consequences of them are my responsibility." Vivienne raised her left eyebrow, showing a hint of an upturn at the corners of her lips. It was a mildly smug look without being condescending.

"Unfortunately, that is an idea too few in this world share." Galin tipped his glass toward her.

He was impressed by her tenacity. She was smart, shrewd, and kind, but she was human. In twenty years or less, he would be forced to leave Italy to avoid detection. It was a life he had led for centuries. It wouldn't be fair for him to get close to her and then leave her without explanation, as her husband had. He would need to keep things casual. Drawing her into his world, burdening her with his affliction, wasn't an option. He found himself thinking of ways he could help her and Vito escape the life they had been forced into without giving her ideas they could be more than friends. He wanted to leave them in a better place than he had found them. Maybe because he had nearly killed Vivienne this morning, he felt an attachment or responsibility of sorts for her. It was exactly the reason he didn't want to involve her in his problems.

But friends they had become. She had asked them all to call her Viv, a nickname Vito had given her as a child when he had been unable to pronounce her full name.

The remainder of the dinner conversation was enjoyable, lasting until the place closed. Galin was in a far better mood than he had been when he arrived in the city that morning. Concluding the evening, they split into their separate groups and returned to their respective lodgings. Dinner conversation had planted an idea in Galin's mind. He waited to voice it until they had returned to their suite.

"Lukkas, what do you think the advantages of having our own bottling facility would be?"

Lukkas rubbed his chin. "With everything we need to master in the production process, I haven't considered it an option. I don't think we're ready for that step just yet."

"I think we should look into it. We spend a lot of money on packaging. If we could bring someone with the knowledge Vito has on board, it may solve some issues for us. Having a completely self-contained operation would prevent problems like we had this morning. We almost didn't get the second half of the shipment to the port in time because it wasn't a priority for our contractor to get our bottles out of their storage facility. If you hadn't paid their extortion fee, we still wouldn't have them." If the numbers were right, Galin thought this would solve two issues. They would control their production from end to end and he would be able to help Vivienne and her brother out of their meager existence.

Lukkas shook his head. "That's a big step, brother. We're in this business for the contacts more than the money right now. What do you think, Grace?"

"I think I'm not going to be dragged into the middle of this." She wagged her finger back and forth between the two men. "I'm not around all the time. I don't mind helping with the manual labor when I'm home, but I'm not comfortable adding my opinion to either argument. With that stated, I bid the two of you a good night." Grace didn't wait for a reply. She exited the main suite for her bedroom and closed the doors that separated the rooms.

Galin should have known Grace wouldn't take a side. She only got between them when they were on the verge of killing each other, which seldom happened. And when things got to the point where she did step in, it was usually not pretty for either brother. They ended the conversation with the agreement that both would investigate the idea.

CHAPTER THREE

Over the next two days, Galin spent his time doing research, looking for information on the complexities of the equipment and the process itself. He visited one of the local bottling factories close to the city, being sure they had no ties to the one Galin and Lukkas had previously contracted with. Using the premise that he may like to look for other bottling options, he was invited by the manager to take a tour. The manager called in the floor boss to show him the operation. When the door swung open, Galin was pleasantly surprised to see Vito standing in front of him. Recognizing Galin, a look of concern flooded over Vito's face.

As the factory manager introduced them, Galin pretended not to know Vito. Vito followed his lead. They left the office, heading down the stairs to the bottling floor.

"Vito, I apologize if my presence disturbed you. I didn't know this was where you worked."

"I have to admit, I thought maybe something happened to Vivienne, and you came to find me. I was relieved you only wanted a tour," Vito chuckled. "Why would you want to tour this place?"

"We're considering bottling on our own. We don't want to continue transporting barrels to locations where we can't control the heat or humidity. It creates too many opportunities to spoil. Our cellar has an area that seems like it was used for bottling previously. We found a few hundred clay containers and large tables. It's rudimentary, but I think it can be adapted," Galin explained.

"Amphorae," Vito said.

"What?" Galin knew what they were from ancient Rome.

"The clay containers. They're called amphorae. No one uses them much anymore. I think that's a shame. They are the perfect vessels for many reasons."

"I'm not sure I understand what you're saying."

Vito chuckled as they took the last steps down onto the floor. "Do you see over there?"

Vito pointed to lines of men with funnels attached to hoses filling bottles with wooden buckets. They stood on platforms, rows of bottles below their feet. They dropped the end of the hose to the bottle and poured wine from the buckets until the bottle was filled up to the spot between the shoulder and neck, an inch below where the cork would sit. Then, once the bottle was filled, someone would come along and drive a cork into the bottle and replace the empty spot on the line with a clean bottle. The filled bottle would then go on a cart for labeling.

Galin nodded. "Yes. It doesn't look as complicated as I had imagined."

"It's not. You take some wine from the vat into a smaller container, fill the bottle and move to the next. Simple." Vito shrugged.

"Go on." Galin was curious about what this had to do with the amphorae.

"Well, they're great for storage and shipping long distances. The clay keeps the wine cool. You wet the outside of the container and it keeps the moisture level high enough." Vito nodded.

Galin nodded back. Vito continued.

"The container is near tall as a man, pointed at the bottom. You tie ropes around the ears, the two big handles on either side of the top. Loop it over a log beam in the ceiling, then tie the rope like a cradle around the pointy bottom."

"So, you have a clay vessel hanging over a beam." Galin thought about traveling on ships. Many amphorae wrapped in rope hung from beams to keep drinking water or wine fresh and cool. Keeping them high out of the way also made more room for cargo.

"Yes. It takes two to lift it into place, but one man can fill many bottles alone. What they do over there, one bucket can fill only a few bottles. It's heavy and awkward to lift. One man fills the bucket, one pours the wine, one replaces the bottle with an empty one and one man presses the cork. That's four men to fill each bottle. It becomes more work than it should be.

"With the amphorae, two men fill the jug; one man fills the bottles, one man presses the cork. Two skilled men can fill nearly as many bottles as four men can here. If you have four men, they can fill twice that. And the wine never needs to leave the cellar. No transportation, no time outside of your control. Less chance it goes rancid or gets moldy before the cork settles. Sometimes the old ways are better."

"That's a lot to think about, Vito."

Galin wanted to test how receptive Vito might be to work with them if Lukkas agreed. He didn't want to seem impulsive or over eager. His thoughts were clearly racing over possibilities as he drummed his fingers on his chest.

Vito had seemed to read his mind. "If you want, I can put together a plan for you. See if you think it's worth setting up."

"As much as I would appreciate your help, I can't possibly take you away from your work here." Galin was pleased with Vito's offer.

"It's no bother at all. This is the last batch we have this week. Should be finished in a few days. Nothing else is scheduled for another week after that. I'd be glad to get out of the city for a couple of days. If you'll have me, that is."

"That's not even a question, Vito. We welcome assistance from a man of your experience. As a matter of fact, you'll come back on the train with us on Saturday. And bring Vivienne. I'm sure she'd be glad to get out of the city for a few days, too."

Vito started to protest. Galin had already surmised he couldn't afford train tickets. Why should he? He was doing them a service.

"Vito, you're doing us a favor. We wouldn't possibly ask you to spend a dime while you're with us. We will pay for your and Vivienne's train passage as well as for your time helping us. I insist." Galin was resolute in his statement.

"Galin, that is a generous offer. Vivienne would be excited at the opportunity to see the countryside again." He paused, nodding his head. "We'll accept the passage. Not another lira aside from that. I insist. Agreed?" Vito held out his hand, appearing just as committed to his words.

Galin could see Vito was a proud man and extended his hand, firmly taking Vito's. "Agreed."

Galin spent the next two evenings with Vito and his sister. They were both knowledgeable about the growing process and production. He was impressed with them. Moreover, he enjoyed the time they spent together. Both were refreshingly open and not at all condescending when he didn't know things they thought he should. Galin genuinely liked them. He had started walking with Viv to drop her day's collections to the fish stand owner after dinner, and then see her home. It gave Vito the opportunity to spend some time alone.

On the third night, Galin had only met Viv for a drink. Galin needed to make an early evening of it. The Board members would be arriving on the northern train for an early meeting the next morning. Viv hadn't dropped off the day's till yet and she wanted to pack for the trip on Saturday. Vito was finishing up at the warehouse and hadn't joined them. They made plans to meet the next night for dinner before Galin watched Viv walk away into the setting sun.

Upon arriving back at the hotel, he was greeted with a pleasant surprise. He opened the door to their suite to see Lukkas sitting in a chair at the far side of the room by the fire. He saw the back of a perfectly coiffed light brown head of wavy hair. As he came around the sofa, Ivan sat at one end and Grace lounged across the remainder of it with her feet in his lap.

Galin nodded, bowing slightly in a formal greeting. "Regent. We weren't expecting you until later. To what do we owe the pleasure?"

Grace pulled her feet back, letting Ivan spring off the sofa. He clapped Galin on both arms firmly.

"Galin, stuff the formality. It's good to see you too." Ivan winked at him. He hadn't been around much in the last fifty years. Ivan was a solitary man, but a very charismatic one as well. He was as close to a brother as Galin and Lukkas had. Seeing him was always a pleasant experience.

Ivan sat back down on the sofa, drawing Grace's feet back into his lap. They were comfortable with each other… maybe a little too comfortable for Lukkas's taste, given the look of envy on his face. Galin took the chair closest to Grace, opposite Lukkas.

"Thought I'd drop in a little early. Spend some quality time with the family." He took a sip out of the glass of scotch he had beside him on the table. "What have you been up to?"

The four had a lengthy conversation about their lives over the last half-century. They caught up on where they had been, business endeavors, and the difficulties the brothers were having with the newly acquired winery. Ivan recounted his adventures visiting other regions, how the community had been evolving, businesses they had gotten into and the political moves they were making. He painted an optimistic picture of their future.

"Wine is an excellent choice. You can go anywhere with that type of business - Chile, Argentina, France, Portugal, and a lot of locations are opening in North America. It's easily inheritable as well." Ivan was always impressed with things you could leave to yourself or a family member every thirty or forty years when you "died". It could also be run through several shell companies, allowing one to transform easily.

"We put a great deal of thought into that," Lukkas nodded.

"Knowing you, Lukkas, I have no doubt," Ivan smirked.

"Why are you really here, Ivan?" Galin asked, leaning back in his chair. He could see there was something else on Ivan's mind.

"You know me too well, Galin." Ivan paused for a moment before he continued speaking. "The Board's plans for our future community includes you taking a more active position if you're up for it."

Galin chuckled. "Well, that sounds ominous. What exactly are you expecting from me?"

Ivan tapped Grace's ankle. "It's more of a long-term plan, nothing that needs to be implemented immediately. You've already seemed to have begun without even knowing it."

Galin felt Ivan was avoiding the question. He leaned forward in his chair. "Ivan. What exactly are you expecting from me?"

Ivan leaned forward, resting his elbows on his knees, trapping Grace's feet against his stomach. Galin wondered if he was using her as a physical ground of sorts. She and Ivan exchanged glances, as if she already knew what he was going to say. Lukkas looked at the two of them with both envy and suspicion, raising his eyebrow.

"We are researching ways to reduce or eliminate the community's reliance on blood."

Galin rubbed his beard, studying Ivan's face intently. "As ambitious as that is, what does that have to do with me?"

"It'll take time. Twenty, thirty or maybe even fifty years before we are able to find a real solution," Ivan spoke cautiously.

"Go on," Galin urged.

"We need someone, you possibly, to set up a worldwide distribution network when the time comes."

"That doesn't sound so difficult, given the time frame." Galin could tell Ivan was still holding something back.

Ivan continued. "No. It doesn't sound difficult. And you will have every resource we can provide. But it will need to be covert. We can't have what we are developing fall into the wrong hands. We can't have it fall into human hands."

"I see. Shipping it with the wine would be something that could be done above suspicion. I don't see where the issue lies here. We can either pay off or entrance anyone who looks too curiously in our direction." Galin still didn't see the difficulty.

Ivan sighed. "Where the issue lies is in the three of you. You've always been part of the community, but you work on the fringes of it. Don't get me wrong; we see that as a good thing. We know you have some less than desirable contacts, and we have no issue with that either. We see how that can be beneficial. Most of us work outside normal parameters in one way or another."

"Ivan! Spit it out!" Galin was becoming irritated with him, dancing around whatever he was trying to get at.

"Establishing a business of that magnitude will place you in a higher profile with humans than most of our community is comfortable with. You'll obviously need to move as you do now every thirty years or so. You will need a larger inner circle to cycle through humanity's memory, but you'll also need to be normal in their eyes. Above reproach. You'll need a family." There it was. Ivan had finally gotten to the point.

"For Christ's sake, Ivan! No. Lukkas and Grace can have kids. They can be the face of the family." Galin was more than irritated. He was pissed the Board would think he would ever consider those terms. Everything they wanted could be accomplished without him taking on a mate and children.

"Galin, you know Grace can't be exposed in that way. We don't know what will happen if she and Lukkas have children. She's not a vampire," Ivan rebutted.

Galin was on his feet, pacing in front of the fire. Ivan went to the bar and poured Galin a glass of scotch from the bottle he had brought with him.

Lukkas had an opinion on the matter as well. "I take exception to the fact that you think Grace and I shouldn't have children. That's not even your business, or the Board's."

"You haven't had any in six hundred years. What makes you believe you even could?" Ivan asked calmly.

"Because I haven't wanted any," Grace snapped. "I still don't want any. I have been here for longer than any of you have existed, but I don't know who I was before or where I came from. Until I can figure that out, I'm not having any." She then turned on Ivan, shaking her finger at him. "And DO NOT talk about me like I'm not in the room."

"You're right Grace, Lukkas. My apologies to both of you," Ivan acquiesced.

Lukkas looked hurt by her remarks, although he kept silent.

Ivan handed the scotch to Galin. Galin slugged it back, shoving the glass back into Ivan's chest.

"Look. It doesn't have to be real. There are plenty of unmated women in the community who would be willing to play the part of your "wife". And as for kids, we have a lot that could pass for teenagers."

Galin shook his head violently. "Ivan, the only thing worse than dragging innocents that I actually care about into this existence is to fake caring about people I don't know. We already live lives filled with lies. I refuse to have the only part of my life that is real distorted in that way."

Ivan went back to the bar to refill both their glasses. "I understand. You know, I still needed to ask. We'll find another way. Would you at least be willing to set up the network? We'll give you as much support as you need. The rest, we can figure out later."

Galin sighed, walking to the bar beside Ivan. He took the scotch and sipped it. It was the first time he tasted it. It was old and smooth. He raised his glass toward Ivan. "You know I can never stay angry with you. I'll set up the network. That's all. Piss on the rest of it."

Ivan clinked his glass back. "Piss on the rest of it."

The men drank, and that was the end of that conversation… and Galin's infatuation with Viv. He needed to find her to ensure she understood before she and Vito made the trip to the winery. There were to be no expectations outside of friendship. It was a conversation that needed to be held between only the two of them. He wanted it to happen tonight before he lost his resolve.

Galin excused himself from the group, telling them he needed to be alone. He soon found himself walking the streets, wondering if what he wanted was what he needed, or if what he was trying to convince himself of was right. Viv was the only woman he found himself thinking about as more than a passing acquaintance in close to a thousand years. Was it right for him to want her in his life, when he hadn't wanted to be what he was in the first place? He had no choice in being born a vampire. If he had been given a choice of being turned, he couldn't even determine now if he would have said yes or no. Would it be fair to think she would know if he gave her one?

No. It wasn't a life he wished on anyone. He wouldn't be selfish enough to offer such a thing to her. It was better this way. It was better for them both. He found himself standing outside her door. Without knocking, he knew she wasn't inside. The pub. She must be at the pub having dinner with Vito. Galin made his way down the familiar street to where he had dined the last few evenings. She wasn't there either. No one had seen her. Where else? Maybe she was taking her evening meal with the fish stand owner's family. A few more blocks until he would find her. Then he would walk her home and ensure she understood their positions.

Her scent wasn't there either. She hadn't gotten this far. He decided to go back to the alehouse where he had met her for a drink earlier. It would be easy to track her from there. Galin readily found her trail. She had walked a block, then he turned toward up the hill toward the fish stand owner's house.

Galin followed her trail toward the alley she often took as a shortcut. The smell reached him from over two blocks away, a mixture of pungent, bitter, and sweet. Blood. Lots of blood. Viv's blood. His heart raced. He felt a sudden, near overwhelming desire to search out the source and drain it. As quickly as the thought came to him, he pushed it out of his mind. He suppressed the thirst, pressing it down deep into an aching urge in his gut. He moved forward, afraid of what he would see.

The alley was dark. It felt damp, reeking of putrid trash, rotting food, and predominately rancid urine. Over all those pervasive odors, the blood drew him. When he stepped into the blackness, he didn't see her. Scanning the area, he found Viv hidden under a pile of trash. Galin pulled it off her. She had been dumped into a crumpled pile in the gutter. Tossed out with common garbage before being covered in her attacker's urine. He could hear her heart beating. As weak as it was, it was beating.

Galin lifted her head. She was unconscious. He fought back the urge to drink from her. He was disgusted by his body's betrayal. His mouth salivated. It would be so easy for him to give in to finishing her off by quenching his own thirst.

Gently, he lifted her. The gash in Viv's stomach opened, spilling out her intestines and darkened blood over her skirt. A small whimpering sound emanated from her throat. Galin held her tightly, speeding through the city, back to the hotel. He wouldn't let her die in that filthy alley. It was no place for someone like her to die. He would take her to Grace so she could die peacefully without pain. It was the least he could do for her.

At the hotel, he laid her on the grass under his window. The leap was too high for him to make with her in his arms. He leapt up into his room, pulled open the door, and yelled for Grace. It was a shocking sight when they saw him covered in blood. Lukkas immediately smelled it was Viv's.

"Galin! What did you do?" Lukkas's eyes were wide, his tone accusatory.

Galin ignored him, snatching Grace by the arm. They were out the window on the ground before she had processed what she had seen.

"Grace, help her. She's dying."

Grace reached out, taking Viv's hand. "I can only take away her pain. You can help her. You can save her."

He was torn. He didn't want to lose her. He could use his blood to heal her, but how would he explain it when she awoke? Would it be enough with her being this close to death? Turning her was something he didn't want to do. It would be selfish to damn her to the life he had.

"Galin!" Grace snapped loudly, slapping his face hard. "Save her or turn her, but don't you dare make me watch her die! I will never forgive you for that."

Grace pulled Viv's pain into her. Viv's eyes fluttered, and she moaned quietly. After a few seconds, her eyes partially opened. Galin leaned over her, lifting her head.

"Galin?" It was barely above a whisper. She tried to smile as she reached up, touching the side of his face. Her hand was icy against his cheek. He covered her hand with his own, holding it against his skin.

"I was so afraid I would die alone. I'm glad yours is the last face I get to see." Viv's head lolled back. Her eyes rolled into her skull and her body went limp.

He was devastated. He should have saved her. He should have turned her. He hated himself for letting her die like that. Then he heard it. One beat. Then another. It wasn't too late. He let his heart take over. She may hate him forever for what he was going to do to her, but it didn't matter. He bit into his wrist, ripping it open. As he pressed it against her mouth, he sunk his canis into her neck and injected as much venom as he had. It poured out of her neck. He didn't know if it was enough. Her heart stopped. She was dead. The unanswered question: would she stay that way?

Relief washed over Grace's face. She knew it had worked. She could feel Viv's human cells dying and the vampire cells spreading through her like an unstoppable virus. She rubbed Galin's back.

"Let's get her up to the room."

"Grace, she's dead."

"She is. But she isn't going to stay that way." Grace smiled warily.

Galin was blank. It wasn't that he had never seen death. He had seen plenty of death. It had just never come so painfully to anyone he cared about. As horrific as his mother's death was, at least it had been quick. He hadn't born witness to his father's death, only the aftermath. Until her body began to heal, he wouldn't believe she was coming back.

They lifted her together easily, making the distance into the window. They laid her in the bathtub where Grace removed her blood-soaked garments, pushed her organs back inside of her, then gently washed her. When she was finished, Grace dressed Viv in a fine nightgown and laid her in Galin's bed. Grace stayed with her, knowing that when she woke, she would need to feed. A small amount of Grace's blood would satiate Viv's hunger. She would care for her and explain what had happened, and what she now was.

While Grace took care of Viv, Galin explained what had happened to Ivan and Lukkas. If it had been any of the other Board members that had come to them, Galin would have questioned their involvement in the incident. If they had been watching him. If they knew he had feelings for Viv, an attack like this would be a calculated risk for them.

Ivan would never be suspect. Not only was he family, but his own turning was also one of the most horrific Galin knew of. It had taken Ivan hundreds of years to come to terms with it. Ivan wouldn't inflict an unwanted turn on anyone.

It had been Ivan who made sure laws were passed so such an event wouldn't go unpunished. It was also Ivan who told Galin he couldn't be exempt and would be required to face the Board in the morning.

"I'm sorry, Galin. I won't be able to protect you from this. There are consequences of turning a human without permission."

"I understand." Galin was still. Ivan could have said they were going to execute him in the morning, and he likely would have had the same reaction. Ivan handed him and Lukkas each a glass of scotch.

"There is some room for mitigation, though," Ivan continued. Galin stood staring ahead.

Lukkas was curious. "How can we mitigate this?"

Ivan pulled Lukkas aside. "Well, if he loves her and was planning on asking for permission to take her as his mate…"

"You want to entrance him." Lukkas paused to consider the implications.

Ivan added, "I want to save him."

"By forcing a lie on him. Did you not hear what he said before he left? He can't live that kind of lie."

"Lukkas, listen. Entrancing can only change memories. It can't make him love her if he doesn't. But, if I make the suggestion, and he does love her, he won't be able to hide it. Not even from himself." Ivan studied Lukkas. His body language was relaxed. His brain had to catch up. Lukkas didn't need long.

"It's worth a try, Ivan. I have one condition, though." Lukkas's mouth was tight, his eyes narrow.

"I don't know if I can promise you anything. What are you asking me for?"

"After you make your suggestion, you and I go hunting," Lukkas sneered.

"Lukkas, you are far more vicious than I gave you credit for."

"It's not revenge, Ivan. It's justice. A justice her attacker will never stand trial for because we can never prove he attacked her after she turns." Lukkas clenched his jaw.

"We'll do it the old way, then. The crime was against Viv. We bring her back his blood and we bring the Board his hand." Ivan needed to be sure Lukkas wanted justice. If he did, it had to be done right.

Lukkas nodded. "Go make your suggestion."

Ivan stood in front of Galin. "Hey."

"Hm?" Galin grunted. His eyes slowly moved to meet Ivan's.

Ivan looked deep, digging into Galin's mind. "You love her, don't you, Galin?"

"I do," Galin replied of his own volition. Pain and guilt cloaked his thoughts.

Ivan hadn't made his suggestion yet. He shrugged at Lukkas. Ivan wouldn't need to go any further. Galin did love her. So much so he thought it would have been better to let her die. His weakness, his selfishness, was what led him to pull her back. It had been his inability to let her go that allowed him to turn her into a vile being like he was. Galin wasn't in shock. He was struggling with his own self-loathing and weakness.

"Galin, you need to get cleaned up, so she doesn't see you like this. Lukkas and I are going hunting."

Galin's upper lip curled into a sneer. "Good." He paused. His eyes hardened. "Gut that prick and let him die alone in the gutter." He stripped off his jacket, pushed past Ivan, and went to take a shower.

CHAPTER FOUR

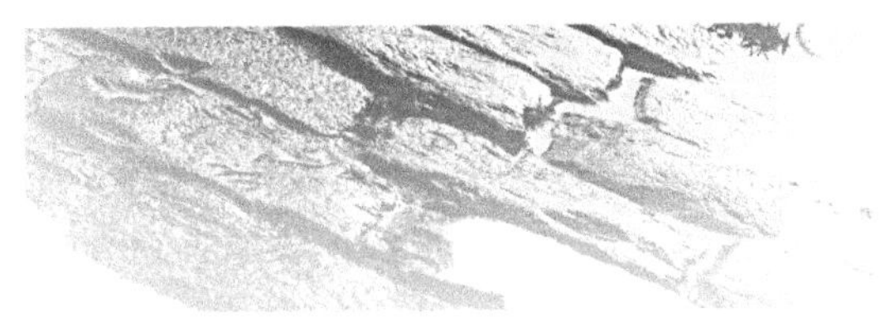

Ivan and Lukkas took Viv's blood-soaked blouse back to the alley where Galin had found her. Blood was everywhere. Viv had fought back hard. Everything for half the length of the narrow corridor was spattered with her blood. Her assailant would be spattered as well. Hunting him would be easy.

"I didn't know he hated us so much." Ivan's words came out of the blue.

"He doesn't hate us, Ivan. He hates the way we are forced to exist." Lukkas understood Galin's struggle.

"I'm going to change that, Lukkas. For all of us."

"I certainly hope you can."

Lukkas knew others in the community had far worse experiences with their affliction than he and his brother did. Galin and he didn't need to hunt for food. They didn't need to drink animal blood or entrance unwilling humans. He and Galin had Grace. She was immortal, but she was human, too. One small dose of her blood could curb the thirst for months. Those who drank from mortals or animals needed to replenish every few weeks. It exposed them. It wasn't safe. Lukkas was grateful for what they had. He couldn't imagine how they would be forced to live otherwise. Their existence was easy compared to most of the community.

They didn't need to track Viv's assailant for long. He was brazen, sitting in the very alehouse where she had met with Galin earlier. Her blood was on his shirt as he drank away the money he had stolen from her. Lukkas was seething. The murderer sat laughing and drinking. He had no remorse for taking a life. In Lukkas's mind, there was no question this man had murdered Viv. She had died by his hand. Now, he would die by theirs. Ivan and Lukkas watched from the shadows across the street. They waited.

Finally, the man emerged with a small group, all of whom were drunk and laughing. A short distance away, the group split apart. Lukkas and Ivan followed the murderer into the alley where Viv had lain. He was leaning against a wall, urinating on a pile of trash covered in her blood. Ivan and Lukkas could smell her there. Lukkas grew livid. This man looked pleased he was desecrating what he thought was the body of a woman he had recently murdered.

"How did you get the blood on your shirt?" Lukkas asked casually, startling the murderer.

The man jerked drunkenly, pissing on his own shoes. "Piss off!" he yelled at Lukkas.

Ivan stood between the man and the entrance to the alley, pulled his whiskey flask out and took a drink. The man eyed it.

Lukkas repeated his question. The man buttoned his pants and turned to face the strangers. He had a black eye and a split lip. His face and neck were scratched and crusted in dried blood. Viv had fought hard. Lukkas smiled at the thought of her getting the better of him until he pulled out a knife. The murderer eyed Ivan's flask. It was expensive, engraved and encased in a leather sheath.

He was smug. "Give me a drink and I'll tell you." He reached out toward Ivan.

"Tell us and I'll give you a drink," Ivan countered, pulling his hand back slightly beyond the man's grasp.

"Some little whore lured me into an alley and then decided she wasn't going to let me have my way. So, I taught her a lesson." An evil pride washed over his face.

Lukkas was nauseous at the idea. It hadn't occurred to him before. He had to ask, even if he didn't want to know. "So, you violated her?"

The man spit on the ground. "No. I taught her a lesson."

Lukkas's nausea subsided. He sneered at the man. "Oh, a lesson?"

"Yeah, a lesson. Now give me that flask."

Ivan held out the flask, slowly tipped it over, and emptied the contents onto the ground. The murderer tried to grab it from him, but Lukkas was so much faster. He had the man against the wall by his throat.

"It's our turn to teach you a lesson," Lukkas whispered, grinning at the man.

The murderer's struggle did nothing against Lukkas's grip. He managed to get an arm around his back, producing the knife he had used on Viv from his belt. Lukkas easily ripped it away from him. He swung it down fast, cutting off the hand. At the same time, he squeezed the man's throat harder, crushing his larynx, stifling the attempts at a scream.

Ivan casually lifted the pulsating stump, pressing it against the mouth of the flask. Once he had filled it, he screwed the cap on and wiped the excess blood on the murderer's sleeve.

Lukkas released his grip. The murderer fell to the ground, cradling his bloody stump. Ivan pulled a piece of leather cloth from his coat, picked up the disembodied hand and wrapped it snugly inside. He callously placed the hand into his coat pocket while the murderer vomited on himself.

Lukkas leaned over the cringing man, attempting to get away from him. He reached into the man's coat pocket and pulled out Viv's money pouch. Lukkas stood back up and tossed the half empty pouch to Ivan.

The murderer must have thought it was over. He scrambled to his feet, trying to run. His inebriated state, coupled with blood loss, didn't allow him to get far. He fell into a pile of trash a few steps further down the alley.

Lukkas scoffed wearily. "Don't make me chase you."

The murder's eyes widened. He tried to beg for his life, but the words wouldn't come out. He scurried backward, blood from his amputated hand spraying over him. Lukkas walked slowly toward him. He crouched down. The stench of fear and decaying garbage had overtaken the odor of alcohol, vomit, and urine. Lukkas smiled down at him, plunging the murder's own knife into his gut. He watched him long enough to see there was no coming back from the attack. He pulled the knife out sideways, allowing the murderer's guts to splay out over his lap. Lukkas laid the knife atop the intestines, stood and joined Ivan at the end of the alley. They looked back to see the horrified look on the murderer's face, and he vomited on himself again as he died.

The pair strolled slowly back to the hotel in unaffected silence.

When they entered the room, the suite was dark. Galin and Grace sat by Viv's bedside. Galin came out to the main room when he heard the two men return. They smelled of blood.

"It's done then?" he asked.

"It is," Lukkas nodded.

"He suffered appropriately?" Galin followed up.

"He did." Ivan took out the flask and the murderer's hand from his coat. He laid the hand on the bar and gave the flask to Galin.

Galin nodded thoughtfully. "Good."

Ivan poured a glass of scotch for each of them. "To justice served."

They drank, refilled their glasses, and moved to the seating area.

"How is she doing?" Lukkas asked.

"She's close. Grace thinks another hour. Her wounds are nearly healed," Galin reported.

"I'm glad it worked on her. It doesn't always take when the blood has been drained like hers was." Ivan's focus had moved off to a corner of the room. Galin thought Ivan was remembering something with either guilt or sadness, maybe both.

They talked for the next hour until Viv began to stir. Grace called Galin in, making the other two wait until she had some bearings about her. Galin was holding her hand when she opened her eyes. She was confused, as he expected she would be. Her turn hadn't been by choice. She hadn't any idea how she had woken up uninjured after such a bloody, violent attack.

"Galin?" Her eyes were wide. She sat up, pushing back against the headboard. She reached down, feeling her stomach. Viv's eyes darted over the room. She sniffed at the air, landing her focus on Grace. Her breathing became heavy, deep, hungry. She lunged toward Grace, who phased, letting Viv plunge through her onto the floor.

Grace was prepared to let her drink, but she wasn't going to let it be an attack. Galin got behind Viv, grabbing her by the waist to hold her back. He hadn't needed to. The shock of passing through Grace brought her back into the moment.

"What is happening, Galin?" Viv pulled back enough to turn in Galin's grasp, facing him.

"We'll explain everything. First, you need to drink." Galin pulled the flask Ivan had given him from his pocket, releasing his grip on Viv.

She had a perplexed expression until he removed the cap. When she caught the scent of the warm liquid inside, she was once again ravenous. She ripped the flask from his hand. Within moments, she had emptied it. The liquid had calmed her thirst. It had settled her, allowing her mind to become her own again. She pulled the flask away from her lips, seeing for the first time what she had been drinking. She was visibly repulsed. Galin took the flask from her shaking hand. He could tell she had an idea what he had turned her into. What she did next surprised him.

Viv took a deep, cleansing breath, straightened herself into her usual controlled posture, grabbed Galin's neck and kissed him on the mouth. She stepped back, ignoring what she had done.

"Now. Tell me what you have done to me," she said, taking a seat in a chair by the fire.

Galin handed her a blanket from the bed, then slowly took the seat beside her. He asked her if she remembered her attack and him finding her. Once they established what she did and didn't remember, he explained the rest of what had happened. Galin hadn't noticed when Grace left the room. Viv was absorbing the information in a clinical manner. She had a number of specific questions Galin hadn't thought of before. He explained that her turn was unusual for their community. Under normal circumstances, an individual was groomed or prepared for the turn. They understood what they were getting into and what to expect. For her, it would be more difficult, and he was sorry for that.

He explained how they differed from the old lore versions used to scare children. They were more susceptible to the effects of sunlight due to their heightened senses, but it didn't set them on fire. A wooden stake through the heart didn't kill them. Anything through the heart was a temporary suspension, wood or not. As soon as it was removed, their bodies would heal themselves. Fire or complete exsanguination was the only way they could be killed. If they had even a drop of blood left, they could reanimate given time. Starvation was exceptionally painful, but they wouldn't die from that either. They would become frail from it, possibly even become insane, but not die. And the biggest difference was that they were not uncontrollable, ravenous animals. They actually preferred not killing to survive. What humans considered food was a pleasure, not a necessity, but it did stave off the thirst somewhat. Alcohol did a better job of reducing the thirst. Most vampires drank at a rate humans would consider excessive.

Viv mostly stared into the fire as he explained. He watched her face for signs of being overwhelmed. She didn't seem to be struggling, but he couldn't be sure how much she comprehended. When he was finished, she turned to look at him.

"Isn't it a basic survival instinct of all animals to kill? Humans kill. Is it better to kill an animal because we don't believe they have the intelligence or the emotions we do? Does it not make our species more evolved that we seek ways not to kill for survival?"

It was more of an existential question than Galin was prepared to debate. To him, it seemed to be a question she needed a simple answer for in order to come to terms with what she had become.

"It shows we are trying to evolve." It was as honest an answer as he could think of.

She contemplated his words, nodding her head. It would be enough for now.

"What about your turn, Galin? How did you handle it?"

"I wasn't turned. Lukkas and I were born this way. He's a few hundred years younger than I am." Galin was one of only a handful of surviving natural born of his age. He had been taught from an early age to hide what he was; to be ashamed of it.

"I didn't know vampires could have children." Viv's eyebrows rose. She found it curious.

"Since the extermination, there are rules about that now. Actually, there are rules about siring someone without permission as well." Galin sighed.

"Siring?" she questioned.

"Turning a human into…" he sighed. "One of us." Galin dropped his eyes to the floor.

"So, you're in trouble. For siring me."

"Yes." Galin didn't want to lie to her.

"What will happen to you?"

"I don't know. There'll be an inquiry. I will go before the Board in a few hours. Don't worry, Viv. No matter what happens, you will always have a place with Lukkas and Grace." He smiled warmly at her.

"If you knew you would be in trouble, why did you turn me?"

He looked away from her into the fire. "I don't know. I just couldn't watch you die."

"I don't believe you."

From the tone of her voice, Galin could tell she already knew the truth.

He turned back to her. "Because I've fallen in love with you." He dropped his head and stared at the floor. "I was selfish. I couldn't let you die even if you didn't return my feelings."

Viv was quiet. She turned back toward the fire. "So, you turned me because you want me to be by your side for eternity? What if that isn't what I want?"

Galin's heart sunk. He felt it drop like a stone into his stomach. He wouldn't make her stay if she didn't want to. "It's your choice. You can ask the Board to help you find another clan where you can be comfortable."

"You would pay the consequences and still let me go if I didn't want to stay with you?"

"Yes."

"But I would always long to be with you because you're my sire. Is that how it works?"

"We would always be connected because I'm your sire. Your feelings are your own. You can love anyone you choose. Do you long to be with me?" Her question had given him the slightest glimmer of hope, forcing him to ask the question.

Viv placed her hand over his. "Galin, you are so dense. I have longed to be with you since you came to find me in the market. Now we have all the time in the world to figure it out. Of course, I'll stay."

Galin sighed deeply before raising Viv's hand to his face. He kissed the back of it. He dared nothing more that she may see as inappropriate.

"We should decide what to tell your brother about last night."

"With everything going on, I'd forgotten about Vito. How are we going to explain any of this to him?"

"It's easiest to stay as close to the truth as possible. I found you after you had been robbed. Brought you back here and Grace took care of you." Galin found it best to offer an explanation as generalized as possible.

"I should go before he leaves for work. He'll be worried." She jumped out of her chair.

"That is not a good idea. Lukkas will go. You need a little exposure to humans before you can walk the streets without wanting to drink them all. We can start with Grace." Viv had only fed a small amount. What was in the flask wasn't enough. Grace's blood would help her more. The first few days would be the most difficult with thirst. The first few weeks would be learning to gain control over the emotions.

"Grace isn't a vampire? How did she do the thing she did?" Galin hadn't explained about Grace or about abilities outside of the physical ones.

"Did she smell like a vampire?"

"She smelled like food." Viv shrugged.

"We're not one hundred percent sure what Grace is, but she's closer to human than not. She is immortal, and she has some abilities the rest of us don't possess. I'm a little embarrassed to say, but she is Lukkas's and my main source of feeding. Her blood is different. We only need a small amount every few months to stave off the thirst. If we fed from other humans or animals, we would need to feed on larger quantities every few weeks. She's not always with us, though. She is blood nurse to all the community's pure born. She's extremely important to our survival."

"I had assumed she was Lukkas's mate," Viv stated.

"It's a little more complicated than that. She is, and she isn't. Lukkas wants to turn her to consider her a proper mate. Grace doesn't want to turn for several reasons. Firstly, she's already immortal and doesn't see the point. Secondly, if she did turn, she wouldn't be able to help the community in the way she does. Besides that, the Board, especially Ivan, would never let Lukkas turn her. He says she is far more important than one man's desire, which I agree with. But, in the end, it's her choice. The community is largely about choice as long as you remain within our laws," Galin explained.

"So, you're saying women have as much choice as men?" This was a novel concept to Viv.

"Yes. Absolutely. Every member of our community is equal. Every vote is equal."

"Women vote?" Viv looked astounded.

"Of course. Many of our clans are even led by women. We all have the same strength. Many have the same abilities. The mind is what is the most important in our leaders. When you've been alive for a thousand or even a few hundred years, you tend to learn a few things."

"How old are you?" Viv scanned him from head to toe.

"Me? Slightly over one thousand."

Viv gasped.

"Well, Ivan is around fourteen hundred. And Grace is older than that."

Viv sat back down. "Years?" It was an unimaginable amount of time to her.

"Yes, years," Galin smirked.

CHAPTER FIVE

Before dawn broke, Lukkas went to Viv's employer, making this visit alone before he saw Vito. He explained what had happened to her and, concerned only about his money, Lukkas launched the remainder of what was recovered from the murderer at him. He scoffed at Lukkas, shaking the pouch.

"This is all? There should be twice this much."

"Well, I'm sorry Vivienne lost half of your money when she was attacked and left for dead alone in a dark alley!" Lukkas yelled out.

The owner puffed out his chest, stepping toward a smaller Lukkas. "You tell her unless she's dead, I expect her to be back at the market tomorrow morning!"

Lukkas then made the unilateral decision to let him know Viv was not returning under any circumstance and he needed to find someone else. Lukkas spat on the sidewalk before marching off indignantly.

His next stop was Vito. Vito was already up and anxious. Viv hadn't cooked breakfast. It was the first inclination he had that she hadn't come home the night before. When Lukkas knocked on the door, Vito jerked it open with widened eyes. He was dismayed to see Lukkas standing in front of him. Lukkas gave him a general breakdown of the events of the night before: Viv had been robbed and injured and Galin had found her and had her attended to. She would be recovering under Grace's care for the next few days. Vito was concerned, wanting to see her as they had expected he would. Lukkas took Vito back to the hotel, where Grace let him see her from the bedroom doorway. Not too close for Viv to catch his scent, but close enough for him to see she was in good hands as she pretended to sleep. Viv had already fed from Grace, but they decided Vito wasn't a human they wanted to test her with. Grace assured Vito if Viv was allowed to rest, she would be able to make the trip back to the vineyard the next day, where she would have time to recover fully. Vito was satisfied and grateful and left for his shift, assuring them he would be back to check on her afterward.

With Vito gone, it was time for Galin to prepare for his inquiry. He was allowed one witness on his behalf. He selected Lukkas, who was also being called forth as Viv's advocate of justice for avenging her murder. It was somewhat convoluted, being that Viv was new to the community. Under their laws, the outright murder of a member allowed their clan to advocate justice on their behalf. Even though her murder had taken place before being claimed by the clan, claiming Viv gave them the right to avenge prior crimes, including her human murder. Fortunately, this law cleared Lukkas of murdering the human, as it was now a right of clan justice. It also didn't hurt to have the Regent himself as his witness. As odd as it sounded, the avenging also gave Galin mitigation for turning

Viv without consent, as he could claim he was going to request permission at the current planned Board gathering, as they were already pressuring him to take a mate. It was the circumstance of her murder that forced him to react outside of their laws. Overall, he had a strong claim.

The Board heard his case. Galin thought it had gone well. He didn't feel any anxiety or negative emotions coming from his jury. After the Board retired to discuss and vote, they returned with an unusual request. They wanted to talk to Viv. Galin had no idea how she would testify or how it would affect the Board's decision. They decided, since she had been turned just twelve hours before, it would be safer for them to go to her instead of bringing her through the human population to report to them. It was a highly unusual procedure. Everything about them being in Genova and coinciding with the incident was highly unusual to begin with. They had originally come to discuss Galin's involvement with the supply network; him taking a mate and starting a family. Galin couldn't help but still be suspicious of their involvement. It bothered him that they wanted to talk to Viv. She was innocent in all of it.

Galin and Lukkas arrived at their hotel suite, nine of the twelve board members in tow. Three were unable to make the journey to Genova. Grace and Viv were in the sitting area where Viv had been peppering Grace with questions all morning. Viv appeared quite controlled when they entered, although Galin suspected she was unnerved by their presence. Five of the nine were women. Only one of the nine did not speak French, Viv's only common language with her clan. Ivan officially chose French for the inquiry, appointing an interpreter to the member who didn't share the tongue. Additional chairs were requested from the hotel staff and, once the members were seated, Ivan made the introductions. Madame Adeline Baptiste had been appointed to question Viv. She took a seat beside Viv, turning the chairs to face each other.

"Don't be nervous, dear. Just ignore them." She waved her hand toward the others on the Board. "I only want to ask you a few questions. You may call me Addie. What is your full name?"

"Vivienne Isabella Costa-Rossi," Viv nodded to Addie.

"So lovely." Addie stroked Viv's hand. "How did you come to meet Galin?"

Viv tittered nervously. "He ran me over with his horse. Before I had even touched the ground, he had me out from under the hooves and on my feet." Her eyes smiled warmly at the memory that seemed so long ago.

Addie smiled bemusedly. "You remember that as an amusing event?"

"Not at the time, of course. I was quite livid with him." Viv leaned forward a bit. "I even swore at him. But now, yes, I find it amusing."

"When was that?"

"It seems like a lifetime ago, although only five days have passed." Viv was beginning to feel mildly uncomfortable with Addie holding her hands. She pulled back a bit, turning toward Galin.

Addie didn't let go. She pulled them closer. "It's all right Vivienne. Look at me. Pretend they're not here."

Now Galin understood. Addie was a reader. She would be able to tell if Viv's words were true.

"So, the two of you haven't known each other long. You haven't spent much time together?" Addie continued.

"No. Time doesn't always matter though, does it? There are some people you have a sense that you've known forever. You know they belong in your life." Viv peered off wistfully for a moment. She turned her gaze back onto Addie. "That probably sounds strange to you, doesn't it?"

"It doesn't sound strange at all. You were drawn to him, then?" Addie asked further.

"I was. It was most peculiar. I tend to keep people at a distance. If you don't let people close, they can't hurt you. I didn't feel I needed to do that with him." Viv showed no emotion on her face.

"I apologize this next question may bring up some difficult memories. When you were attacked and awoke to see him looking down at you, what were your thoughts?" Addie scrutinized Viv's expression.

"I was glad his would be the last face I saw before I died. I think I even said that to him." Viv's features were relaxed, soft. Her expression was calm.

"Did you know what he was?"

"No."

"But you understand now?"

"Yes."

"If he had asked you if you wanted the turn when you were dying, how would you have answered?" Addie's question was difficult for Viv to answer appropriately. She took a moment to phrase her words.

"At that specific time, I can't say I had enough information to adequately answer yes or no. I don't know if I would have understood what he was asking me. In retrospect, knowing what I now know, I would have told him yes. My only regret was that we didn't have more time to prepare. It was an urgent situation and I do not regret that he made that decision for me." Viv scrutinized Addie's face, which gave nothing away.

"Are you willing to take him as your mate, then?" Addie pushed.

Viv pulled back into a stauncher posture. "I am willing to take him as my partner. The term mate has a connotation of being a breeding pair. I think the two of us alone should decide if we are willing to procreate."

Addie looked to Galin as if she was choking back laughter. She released Viv's hands, turning to the Board members, many of whom appeared to have enjoyed Viv's answer.

"I believe we have all the answers we need." Addie placed her hand on Viv's knee. "Thank you for your forthright honesty, Vivienne."

Ivan stood up. "Please, give us a few moments to discuss the issue."

Galin nodded to Ivan. He, Lukkas, Viv, and Grace went into the adjoining room. Galin turned to Viv.

"I am so sorry you had to go through that." He moved in to embrace her.

Viv placed her hand on his chest, holding him at an arm's distance. "Do not treat me like I am in any way the type of weak woman you are accustomed to dealing with. Our relationship is not going to be that of mates. I meant what I said. We are partners. We have a lot to learn about each other, and it is going to begin with mutual respect." She scrutinized his bewildered expression.

"But what you said. I mean…"

Viv cut him off. "Everything I said was truthful. This situation is beneficial for both of us. I do have feelings for you, but I am not going to let my emotions overtake my sense. We are quite equal in intelligence and passion. I suggest you not forget that. This is all new to me. We have nothing if not time to create something between us in the right way. Now, I would appreciate if you would maintain a morally appropriate distance that a respectable single woman requires in this society. Especially in public."

"You're right. I was presumptuous. Appearances are vitally important in this narrow-minded environment. I have a vast amount of respect for your position. I agree we should pace ourselves appropriately. My apologies." It had been a very long time since Galin had been put in his place by anyone. It was refreshing she was comfortable enough to do so. It made him like her even more.

"Now, since we're not in public," Viv kissed Galin on the cheek, making him blush. "Thank you." She brushed down the shoulders of his suit and straightened his tie. "Tell me what punishment we should expect from them." Viv stepped back and flopped down on the edge of the bed, leaning back on her elbows.

Galin smirked at her. "You are quite the conundrum, woman."

Viv smirked back at him. "Yes. That I am."

Galin looked back to see Lukkas and Grace grinning at them. He shook his head. "Honestly, I don't know what to expect. They seemed to like your testimony. I'm not sure what they would believe to be an appropriate punishment."

Galin wasn't being fully truthful with her. Punishment for turning without approval could be quite harsh under certain circumstances. He felt they had a good argument and Viv had shown herself to be of quality. She would make for an excellent addition to the community. The Board would take her potential into consideration as well.

"Well, whatever it is, we'll deal with it when it comes." Viv was pragmatic.

"We will," Galin echoed.

"What was that whole hand holding thing Addie was doing all about?" Viv wiggled her fingers in the air, scrunching up her nose.

"Oh that? She's a reader," Grace answered.

"You mean like crystal balls and candles?" Viv said cynically.

Grace snorted. "No. Most of those types are con artists. Vampire abilities are enhanced from what you already had as a human. If you are sensitive to energy or telepathy, then the gifts are greater after the turn. It's the same way your vision, hearing and smell become enhanced. Addie was sensitive to emotions before. Now, she's somewhat of a living lie detector. She only needs to touch the person to tell."

"So, it's like the way you can control the movement of energy to pass through objects." Viv raised her eyebrows.

"I'm not sure that's a similar comparison because I never turned, and I don't know if I've always had the ability. But, yes, it's an ability outside of the normal human range." Grace tried to explain.

"What abilities do the two of you have?" Viv nodded between Lukkas and Galin.

Galin answered. "For Lukkas, it's always been math. He can extrapolate complex equations in his head. And he's a true magician with money."

"What about you?" Viv asked Galin.

"I'm not extraordinary. I don't have any gifts."

"He's being modest. He has an extraordinary business acumen. Seems to always know how to cultivate a deal to his advantage. He's very good at getting ahead of an issue before it becomes a problem." Lukkas spoke proudly of his brother.

"That's not a gift. I put in a lot of time and effort to research my subject before I make a proposition. That's all." Galin downplayed his achievements as he rolled his eyes at Lukkas.

Viv shrugged. "Even if you don't think of it as a gift, it is an ability most don't have."

"I guess."

"I wonder if I have any abilities," Viv wondered aloud.

Galin wanted to say control, organization, unpredictability and terrifying people, but decided to keep it to himself. "We'll have to wait and see," he ultimately answered.

There was a knock on the door. Viv was on her feet before it opened. It was Ivan.

"We're ready for you."

The four exited the room apprehensively. Lukkas, Grace, and Viv took seats set up to the side of the Board. Galin stood in front of them facing the Board, throat dry and having difficulty swallowing. Galin usually wasn't the nervous type, but this punishment would affect more than just him.

Ivan stood in front of the Board facing Galin. "Galin Eliassen, you have been found guilty of the charge of the unlawful turning of a human. We have concluded that we, the Board, in part, contributed to your actions. We made requests of you that may have set your course of action. Had we not made our presentation when we did, you would not have altered your plans to escort Mademoiselle Rossi after your meeting, on her way through the streets of the city. Mademoiselle Rossi would not have been alone in the alley for her attacker to happen upon. You would not have found her in the state she was in, forcing you to make the decision you did. We further believe you would have, in your own time, requested approval from the Board to have Mademoiselle Rossi evaluated for the turn. That is not to say your actions were not rash and unlawful. You will be required to be held responsible for those actions. Do you understand and agree?"

"Yes. I am ready to take responsibility for my actions," Galin spoke humbly.

"For your crime, you will be held fully responsible for Mademoiselle Rossi for a term of fifty years. Any actions or infractions she is deemed guilty of, you will bear her full sentence. Do you understand?" Ivan paused.

"Yes," Galin answered.

"Furthermore, you are solely responsible for Mademoiselle Rossi's education on our community, culture, and laws. Do you understand?"

"Yes," Galin responded again.

"Lastly, you will be required to participate in the requested action set forth by the Board last evening. Do you understand?"

Galin had already resolved to set up the supply network. He had no choice but to agree. The normal punishment for turning someone without permission was the forfeiture of the newly turned member's life. He understood he was getting off with a light sentence. The only thing that mattered was that Viv would be allowed to live. He would have gratefully accepted any sentence short of that.

"Yes, I understand."

Ivan turned back to address the Board members. "This concludes the inquiry, verdict, and sentencing for community member Galin Eliassen on the charges of unlawful turning of a human. Do I have any objections to the closing of this inquiry?"

No one objected.

Ivan nodded. "This inquiry is closed. Board members, thank you for your participation. This meeting is adjourned."

Once the Board members had welcomed Viv into the community, one by one they left. Only Ivan remained. He apologized he couldn't get Galin off with probation. He did get him the lightest sentence everyone would agree to. A few members thought Galin should be made an example of, to discourage others from attempting the same thing. Galin was not only an important member of the community, but was one of the oldest.

Galin was grateful for the limited sentence he had received. He understood what could have happened. When it was all over, Lukkas and Ivan decided to take Grace to lunch, giving Galin some time alone with Viv.

Grace had given Viv a lot of information that morning. There were many more things she couldn't answer, mostly about how it was different from being human. Grace had no real experience with either state of existence. She hadn't been weak or mortal and she hadn't had to experience shifting through heightened senses. She could tell Viv how they had felt to her from the outside, but Grace had no way to convey the internal feeling.

Honestly, Galin couldn't relate to that experience either being pure born. He knew how he felt. And he had seen others go through the process, but it was still foreign to him. He took Viv out onto the balcony so he could see how the sun, scents, and sounds were affecting her. Galin handed her a pair of smoky quartz crystal spectacles he had purchased in China nearly one hundred years earlier.

"I'm not wearing those. People will think I suffer syphilis." Viv was appalled at his suggestion. She would rather suffer the brightest rays of the sun than the scorn of people in the streets.

"Suit yourself. You'll get used to it. The first two or three weeks are the worst for your new sensitivities. We'll wait until this evening to go out."

"Going out? Are you sure it's safe?" Viv questioned.

"For you or for them?" Galin joked.

"Ha. Ha." She wasn't amused.

"You shouldn't have a thirst. You fed this morning. The only thing I worry about is your temper. Grace and Lukkas are coming with us, anyway." Galin started rethinking that statement before he had finished it.

"What's that supposed to mean?" Viv squinted at him.

"Um, which part?"

"My temper?" Viv's expression hadn't changed. She cocked her head to the side and folded her arms.

"Not you specifically, Viv. All newly turned in general have some work to do in controlling their emotions. It's not uncommon to have a mild outburst of anger or melancholy." Galin hoped he was digging himself out and not further in.

"Uh-huh. And you think you need Grace and Lukkas to control me?"

"Oh no. Just Grace. Remember how she took away your pain? She can give it back in spades, rendering you unconscious before you can open your mouth. You won't have the opportunity to embarrass yourself. She's done it to Lukkas and me on more than one occasion."

Further in. He was definitely digging further in.

"So now you think I'm going to embarrass myself?"

Galin threw his hands up and stepped back. "I yield."

Viv burst out laughing. "I was kidding. I really love twisting you up." She dropped her arms as she sighed. "Galin, stop walking on eggshells around me. If you have something to say, say it. Just like you would have before. You're not going to offend me, but you are going to piss me off if you keep tiptoeing around me like that."

"All right. No tiptoeing. Just remember you asked for that."

"I will."

"Okay. Let's start with the obvious things. What can you see?"

"It's bright. Like someone holding a lamp up in your face. Everything is whitewashed in the light. Colors are muted as if I am seeing them through snow." Viv was squinting again.

"Turn so your back is to the sun, then tell me what you see."

"The colors are brighter, but it all still appears foggy. That isn't right. I don't know how to describe it." Viv was frustrated.

"No, that's good. What you're seeing are particles. Dust, pollen, tiny particles suspended in the air. Focus on them. You'll see them for what they are."

"Oh, you're right. I didn't know so many things hung in the air." Viv sounded excited.

"Good, now shift your focus past them to something in the distance. One thing, anything you want." Galin came close behind her.

"There's a woman at the caffè past the walking bridge. She's wearing red." Viv pointed up the street.

Galin moved as close as he could without touching her. He placed his hand on the rail and followed the line of her arm to the woman down the street.

"Concentrate on her. Can you see her tie pin? Her shoe buckles?"

"Yes! Oh my gosh. Yes, I can see everything."

"Seeing is much more precise than looking. Viv, that woman is nearly a mile away."

Viv gasped, leaning back against Galin. She was, for the first time since he had met her, at a loss for words.

"Close your eyes and tell me what you hear."

Viv placed her hand over his on the rail to keep her balance when she closed her eyes. She pressed her weight against him. He placed his free hand on her upper arm as she sunk deeper against him. He closed his eyes.

"Everything is so loud. I can hear the bells at the port. I hear so many people talking, horses' shoes on the street, motorcars, silverware clanging, the wind whispering. Loudest of all, I hear your heartbeat." She was swaying with his breathing.

He whispered in her ear, "What about your heartbeat?"

"I only hear yours." Her breathing was in rhythm with his.

"Listen closer. Concentrate. Make all the other sounds go away," he whispered more softly.

"Ah, now I hear. They're beating at the same time, yours and mine," she spoke softly.

"They are."

"Is that normal?"

"I don't think so." He didn't know. Maybe it was because they were so close and relaxed. He hadn't paid attention to others before.

She took a deep breath, relaxing even further. "Before you say anything. I'm not doing smell. It's already disgusting enough without concentrating on it."

He chuckled, shaking them both. She was right. The city smells were disgusting. He preferred the country. The city reeked of trash, rotting fish, smoke fumes and horse shit. At least the animal feces in the country wafted by occasionally. In the city, it was constant with so many animals confined in such a small area.

Viv spoke in a low, relaxed tone. "I can smell the blood, too. Animal blood mostly. I can smell it coming from the south. From the market and the butcher shops."

"How does that make you feel? Do you need it?"

"No. I want it. I can trace it through the streets. I can see which way I need to turn to get to it with my eyes closed. But I don't need it. Not right now, at least." Viv hadn't moved from her comfortable position against Galin's chest.

"Let one of us know if that need gets too strong. That's your thirst. You can't let it get to the point where you can't control it. Okay?"

She turned to face him, placing her head against his shoulder. He didn't expect it. "Can we go back inside? It's difficult out here."

"Of course. You did very well for your first time outside. Are you tired?" Galin was exhausted himself.

"I could use a nap before we go out later," she answered. "You didn't sleep at all last night, did you?"

"No, fortunately, we only need a few hours of sleep. I'll take the sofa. You can have the bed," Galin offered.

"That's silly. The bed is huge. You sleep on top of the blankets; I'll sleep under them."

"Your brother will be here after his shift to check on you. Do you not think he would see that as inappropriate?" Galin didn't want to argue about it. She was the one who needed the appearance of propriety. As far as the community was concerned, they were already paired.

"You'll be up and at the door before he ever gets off the elevator. Besides, Grace and Lukkas will be back before he gets here. We can leave the bedroom door open." Viv went into the bedroom, pulling her scarf down as she went.

Galin stood watching her as she took off her over dress, leaving her corset and under dress in place. She climbed onto one side of the bed.

"Are you going to stand there gawking at me, or are you going to get some sleep?" Viv rolled on her side, facing the middle of the bed, and closed her eyes.

Galin pulled the drapes shut before he hung his jacket on the side chair. He removed his vest, shoes, tie and cuff links, turned out the lamps, and laid on his back on the other side of the bed. When he closed his eyes, he felt her watching him.

"Are you going to lie there gawking at me, or are you going to get some sleep?" He quipped.

"I think I'll gawk for a minute," she replied sleepily.

Viv felt a breeze of air across her face. She had sensed Lukkas and Grace return to the suite earlier. It had been an odd sensation just under her consciousness. She hadn't fully woken up until now. When her eyes opened, Grace was sitting where Galin had been sleeping. Viv could hear him dressing behind her.

"Vito's coming up." Grace had a book in her hand. "Close your eyes."

Viv did as she had been told. She could hear footsteps echoing from the far end of the hallway outside the suite, the heavy steps of a large man. The scent of sweat and wine was familiar to her. She lay motionless as Vito rapped lightly on the door. Viv slipped her eyelids back far enough to peer through her thick eyelashes. Lukkas opened the door, exposing a worried Vito. She heard Galin slip into the chair beside the bed, propping his feet on the corner near hers. Between him and Grace, they were the picture of concern standing watch over an injured friend. Grace shot her an unexpected jolt of pain, forcing her to squeeze her eyes shut tight.

"Come on in Vito. She's sleeping," Lukkas whispered.

To Viv, his voice was as loud as if he was standing mere feet away.

"Thank you for seeing to her. How's she doing?" Vito shuffled his hat through his hands.

"The doctor came earlier. She hasn't any permanent damage. She does need rest. The fresh air in the countryside will do wonders for her." Lukkas was doing what he could to convince Vito not to pull out of the trip.

"What about the train? Won't that be hard on her?" Vito's voice wavered.

"The train is comfortable. We can have a lounge brought into our compartment for her if she needs it. She'll do much better once she's out of the city," Lukkas answered.

"But what about her injuries?" Vito protested.

Lukkas pulled Vito over to the bar, pouring them both a drink, when Galin joined them. Lukkas deferred the question to Galin.

"Vito, we are more concerned about her emotional health. Her physical injuries are minor in comparison. She was attacked in a place where she has always felt safe. She's afraid of being alone right now. She wakes often in a state of panic. We've been told it won't be uncommon to expect mood swings from anger to melancholy. She will benefit from being somewhere we can all make her feel safe again."

"Viv is a strong woman. I've seen her tossed around before. She always takes it on the chin." Vito needed a little more convincing.

Galin placed his hand on Vito's shoulder. "Vito, that man didn't only rob her of her money. He robbed her of her confidence. She felt vulnerable. He knocked her unconscious. He could have done anything to her if he had wanted to, and she knows that. I didn't find her until well after."

Vito gave Galin a suspicious glance. "How exactly did you find her, Galin? I thought you had a meeting last night."

"I did. It ended early, so I went to the tavern to see if the two of you were having dinner. Neither of you had been there. Something didn't feel right to me. I went to her employer's residence and, when she hadn't shown up there, I went looking for her. I knew roughly the route she would have taken from the pub. It didn't take long after that to find her. Didn't you notice her missing?"

Galin threw the accusation back on Vito. After all, he didn't notice she hadn't come home until morning. He didn't know she had been attacked until Lukkas had gone to fetch him.

Vito shook his head wrought with guilt. "No. There was a problem at the warehouse. I didn't get home until after midnight. Her door was closed. I thought she was asleep."

"She's safe now. That's what matters, isn't it?" Lukkas interjected.

"I never meant to sound ungrateful. You're good friends. I'm glad it was you that found her," Vito said.

Galin frowned. "I am too. I only wish I had found her earlier. She wouldn't be going through this now. Your sister is a special woman, Vito. She'll get through this."

Galin spoke his heart. He did wish he had found her earlier. There was no regret in saving her. His regret was that he had needed to turn her to do it.

"I don't know how special she is, but she is all the family I have left." Vito bowed his head, shuffling his feet. Galin's admiration of Viv was apparently an uncomfortable subject for Vito.

Viv rolled onto her back with a soft whimpering sound. The motion had its intended purpose of shifting their focus away from the conversation. Grace responded, placing the back of her hand on Viv's forehead, then lightly stroking her hair.

"Shhh." Grace shushed the men. "Let her sleep."

"We should probably go down to the bar," Galin whispered.

Vito replied, "I don't want to cause any trouble. I should be going. I still need to pack a bag. Should I pack for Viv too?"

"Don't worry about all that. Grace has plenty of things Viv can wear. Trust me, more than enough. She brought three trunks this week alone. And she bought a dozen more dresses since we got here." Lukkas tightened his jaw, rolled his eyes and held them shut a few seconds to pronounce his exasperation with the sheer quantity of Grace's wardrobe.

Grace bit her tongue. Who could blame her? When a lady is required to change four times a day to keep up appearances of old money and high society, she needs a sizable wardrobe. Men could wear one suit the entire day, only changing for evening dinner or theater. If it had been up to her, she'd be wearing riding pants or a linen skirt and shirt all day like she did at the vineyard. She certainly wouldn't be trussed up in a boned corset to the point where she could barely take a breath.

"Well, I should be going." Vito shifted his weight. "I don't know how I can repay you for taking care of her. It means a lot to us."

Galin put his hand on Vito's shoulder. "She's important to us too, Vito. Real friends don't need to be repaid. Ever."

Vito nodded uncomfortably. "See you in the morning."

"The train leaves at ten. We'll meet you at the station at nine-thirty." Galin patted him on the shoulder, guiding him toward the door. "Have a good night, Vito."

"Good night." Vito left the suite looking much calmer than he had been when he entered.

Once he left, Viv sat up. "Well, that was sad. I really don't like lying to him."

Grace shut her book. "Would you like me to bring him back? You can tell him everything."

Viv glanced at her sideways, ignoring the comment. "So, where are we eating tonight? I'm starving."

Grace hopped off the bed. She went to her room, bringing back two dresses out of her closet. "Well, you're not going in that. Red or black."

Viv's eyes widened. Either of the two choices would pay her rent for six months. "Grace, I couldn't."

"Of course you can. And you need to get used to it. Red? Or black?" She held each choice forward as she enunciated the color.

Galin studied Viv as the thought sunk in. She wouldn't ever be going back to her old life. She was theirs now.

"Red," Viv said, throwing back the covers. She took the dress from Grace, walked toward Galin, and shut the door in his face as he stared at her.

Nearly two hours later, they were standing outside of the most exquisite restaurant Viv had ever laid eyes on. It had taken Grace and Viv a little time to let the hem out on the dress, since Viv was so much taller than Grace.

"Are you ready?" Galin asked, squeezing her hand looped through his arm.

She stared off at the doors. "So many tasty things in there," she replied in a disconnected way. She ran her tongue slowly over her top front, teeth brushing the bottom edge of her upper lip.

Galin smiled at her. He put his finger under her chin, pulling her face toward his.

"You'll be fine. You can have all the champagne you want," he teased.

"Champagne goes straight to my head. Are you trying to get me inebriated?"

"It doesn't work like that for you anymore."

"Well, that's a shame. I don't have any excuse to let my staunch morality slip, do I?" Viv whispered back.

"Vivienne Rossi, are you flirting with me?" Galin asked at a barely audible level.

"If you must ask, I must not be doing it right," Viv replied as she stepped in front of him.

"Oh no. You're doing it right," Galin whispered over her shoulder. He guided her forward as the doorman held open the door.

He was a little concerned with Viv's behavior. It could be the sire effect. Since she was his first, it was difficult for him to be sure. It could also be that she was experiencing some emotional instability. It was common to have swings from euphoria to rage. The only other thing he could think of was she was experiencing real freedom for the first time in her life. Whatever it was, it was clear she was feeling very good this evening. Galin would make sure he kept a close eye on her.

Dinner lasted three hours, which was average at this establishment. It went as well as could be expected. Light conversation without major incident. The biggest issue of the evening had been which fork to use for the shellfish.

After dinner, Galin had concluded Viv was well in control of her actions. He attributed her giddy demeanor to her internal ability to maintain control of herself, paired with the calming effects of Grace's blood. Keeping to light topics had also been a good choice for the evening. She was faring far better than he had expected.

They decided to walk back to the hotel. It was dark except for a few streetlights dotting the landscape in front of them. Temperatures had dropped and a cool breeze was blowing from the sea. The air was laden with a salty mist, creating a halo effect around the moon and streetlights. Viv's eyes darted from dark corner to dark corner. Galin could see she was in a heightened state of alert.

He was impressed that she didn't panic. After the incident, he wasn't sure what reaction to expect from her. The real challenge would be ahead. There was an unlit stretch of road yet to pass through. Galin readied himself to hold her back if necessary.

With her new ability to see in the dark, Viv's confidence appeared unchallenged. She didn't look nervous to him. She looked somewhat like a predator scanning every inch attentively, listening for unusual movement. He watched her nostrils flair, taking in the scent of the air. The vision of a panther crossed his mind. Sleek, dark and stealthy. Galin wasn't sure why he had thought of that image. The comparison fit.

Upon arriving back at the suite, Viv was exhilarated. The journey hadn't scared her at all. It had awoken her.

"That was liberating." She poured herself a glass of wine, offering the bottle to the others.

Grace held out an empty glass, joining her. "The meal or the walk?"

"The power," Viv replied.

Galin was astonished by her words. He didn't see her as the type to revel in aggressive behavior.

"Oh, I see that look, Galin." Viv eyed him up and down. "I meant the power to take back my own freedom from fear. To walk the streets alone, knowing I will never go through what happened to me in that alley. To know I can't be hurt like that again. You don't understand because you've never been weak. None of you have."

"No, we've never been weak, but we have been hunted. We've lost many to human fear. You have advantages of strength and enhanced senses now. Don't mistake that for safety." Galin needed her to understand she couldn't be flippant about exposing herself.

"Galin, let me have my moment of confidence. Do you think me so daft as to believe I would risk exposing the community for a thrill? Do you know me to be careless or reckless? You told me the turn doesn't change a personality; it only enhances it. What are you so afraid of being enhanced in my personality?" Viv stared him down.

"Nothing."

"Then why don't you trust me?"

"It's not you. I'm not certain of what emotional affects you are going through, what mood swings you may have as a result of the turn." Galin was attempting to explain what was making him so cautious around her. The bottom line was, he really didn't understand what she was feeling.

"Then ask me, Galin. And stop lecturing me." Viv took a sip of her drink. She turned back toward Grace. "This is quite lovely. Is it one of yours?"

"It's one of ours," Grace replied, lifting her glass.

"One that was previously produced or one from a current harvest?" Viv continued being inattentive to Galin, who was left stunned silent.

"Previous. We've only recently taken our first harvest," Grace answered.

Galin interjected, "Are you going to simply ignore me, Viv?"

"I'm not ignoring you, Galin. I've only made a choice to end an unproductive line of conversation. You don't trust me. I have no recourse in challenging an unfounded idea. Hence, I ended the discussion. You need to work out your trust issues on your own."

"Viv, that might be just a tad bit harsh," Grace spoke from behind her. "He has so little experience with women's moods and feelings in the first place. And now you expect him to understand one who he's recently turned?"

"Grace, I don't see how it's my responsibility to help him work that out. He should be able to trust the fact that I'm not going to let my emotions overcome my sense." Viv was now turned sideways between the two.

Galin stepped forward. "It's not your responsibility. And in a perfect world, we would have known each other for years before you took the turn. So, yes, I am having difficulty separating your baseline emotional responses from the effects of the turn. It's also not that I don't trust your sensibilities. I've seen perfectly sane people have wild outbursts of temper and physical violence in the beginning. It isn't something you will be able to control once it starts to escalate. Trust has nothing to do with it."

"You're monitoring me, then?"

"Yes. Which is why I asked you to let me know if you feel anything unusual." Galin couldn't understand why she was being difficult about it. He hadn't asked her to do anything illegal or immoral. He had only asked her to report her emotional state to him.

"Galin," Viv took a step in his direction. "I think it would be much less stressful to leave the monitoring duties to Grace." She turned, nodding to Grace. Grace nodded back. Viv looked back at Galin. "You and I would be better off working toward getting to know each other."

Galin was relieved at her suggestion. He would much rather enjoy being with her than evaluating her temperament every second. "I must agree. Grace is far better suited to track unusual activity with you than I am. It would be a relief to not have that responsibility."

"You see her better suited because she's a woman?" Viv side eyed him, raising an eyebrow again.

"As vexing as you are attempting to be, I'll not let you bait me into that argument. She's more qualified because she can feel your entire being." Galin smiled at her.

Viv smiled broadly back. He found her aggressive dry humor appealing. He would need to be quick and keep his wits about him at all times with her. Otherwise, he had the feeling she would be able to verbally castrate him within seconds.

"Excellent answer." She handed him her glass. He took the final drink from it and refilled it, handing it back to her.

"Thank you, Galin. I should have you domesticated in no time." He chuckled at her statement. She continued. "Think of me as one of your contracts. You have made the offer. I have accepted. All that's left is to navigate the terms."

"What if you decline my terms?" Galin asked.

"Then you reconsider your terms. It's a negotiation, Galin. We compromise, like with every other contract you've written."

Viv was nothing if not practical. Galin realized she hadn't picked her new life, but he could see she was going to take advantage of her new circumstances. He would do the same if given her position.

"Well, you've given me a lot to think about, haven't you?"

Grace stepped up to the pair. "On that note, we have an early morning followed by a very long day of travel. I suggest we retire for the evening."

"I, for one, think that's a grand idea." Lukkas spoke for the first time since they had begun this conversation. He headed toward his room with Grace.

Grace caught him by the arm. "You're sleeping with Galin. Viv is sleeping with me."

"But…" Lukkas stammered.

Galin put his arm around Lukkas's shoulder, pulling him toward the other bedroom. "Pick your battles, Lukkas."

CHAPTER SIX

Five thirty seemed to come late. Viv had already been up for an hour. Galin watched her as she sat on the balcony, taking in the early morning rush of vendors to the market. It was overcast, clouding the light of the moon. The sun was beginning to shift the hue to a dark purple on the horizon. The color transition was subtle. It would be another hour until sunrise. Galin could hear the ships pulling into port with their catch. This was the time of morning Viv would usually head down to the pier to pick out her catch of the day for the fish stand.

A short time later, the maids came up to pack them for the trip, bringing a new style of coffee they called cappuccino. Galin hadn't tried one before. Viv called it a breakfast coffee and had ordered one for each of them. Grace couldn't get enough of the coffee and milk concoction topped with chocolate and cinnamon. That was no surprise, seeing that Grace couldn't pass up coffee in any form at any time of day or night. Galin wasn't happy having extras added in and would be sticking with a simple caffè lungo or a french press when he was at home. Lukkas was non-committal. He preferred tea with honey to any coffee drink and gave Grace his cup to finish.

Washed, dressed for travel, and packed up - the bags headed to the train station, while the foursome headed to the hotel restaurant for breakfast. It was the last stop before they would finally be on their way home.

The train station was the most difficult challenge for Viv. The sheer volume of people packed into such a confining space was not only enticing but also claustrophobic. Grace felt Viv's panic rise. She was surrounded by food and afraid. Not a good combination in a new vampire. Grace pulled her into an upper-class ladies' lounge with a much lower congestion level. They paid the attendant for a private sitting room until they could board the train.

Viv was breathing slow and deep, scrambling to regain some sort of composure. Grace pulled off her gloves. She pulled Viv's off too, grasping her forearms. Viv felt a warm, comforting sensation moving up her arms into her core. Her breathing eased as her body relaxed. Her jaw unclenched. Grace could see Viv's canis retracting from the outline under her upper lip. She could see the anxiety was painful for Viv, so Grace began to pull her pain away like the night Viv had been murdered.

"Leave it. I need to feel it." Viv winced. When it was only the two of them, Viv was more comfortable speaking in Italian.

"You need to feed. There are too many people here."

Viv nodded. "I know I should. I don't want to lose control out there. Why don't I feel as compelled to rip your throat out and drink you dry as I do with them? I wanted to right after I woke after the turn. I tried to attack you."

"I don't have any idea. It's not like you could drink me dry. I'm a bottomless blood supply." Grace grinned impishly. "That, and you can't touch me if I don't let you."

"True. It's something else, though. Your presence is soothing." Viv sighed. "Well, what's the cleanest way to go about this? Can't walk out there with blood all over the dress."

"Sit down." Grace pulled out a large, dark-colored handkerchief and held it under her wrist in front of Viv's mouth. "Drink. And try not to venom me. I despise having numb fingers."

Viv held Grace's arm and slowly sank her teeth into the wrist. Grace noted she fed much more cleanly than the boys did. Viv didn't spill a drop. She only drank until she was satiated, then pulled off slowly, which Grace also noted as unusual. Newly turned, usually fed rabidly and had to be forced off. Grace thought Viv's feeding was much more ladylike, for lack of a better term. It was as if she was feeding more for comfort than for thirst.

"Better?" Grace asked.

"Much. Thank you," Viv answered, holding out her own arm. "Here, take some of my blood to heal your wounds."

Grace wiped her wrist with the cloth, raising it to show perfectly unblemished skin. "No thanks. All gone."

"I don't know why that surprised me. What are you anyway?" That was a conversation she and Grace hadn't gotten into yet.

"Don't know." Grace shook her head slowly, shrugging.

"How old are you?"

"Don't know that either. At least sixteen hundred that I know of. But I think I was already old before that." Grace scrunched her brows together, dropping the corners of her mouth into a slight frown.

"What makes you think that?" Viv asked, slipping her long gloves back on.

Grace thought that was an unusual question. No one had ever asked her why. "I'm not sure. It's a feeling locked in my bones. I had a family. I had sons. Three. I'm sure of it. I dream of them through a mist. Like watching someone else's memories. I can't see their faces. I dream of hearing them sometimes too. I can hear them calling out to me." Grace's voice drifted, as did her focus. She stood straight, clearing her throat. "You must think I've gone mad. Please don't repeat any of that to Lukkas or Galin. I'm certain they would fear for my sanity."

"If that isn't the pot calling the kettle black. How is any of this sane? We consume blood to survive. Every living being consumes something else to survive. You, from what I can see, consume what? Anger? Fear? Pain? You survive on the worst parts of others, yet somehow manage to convert all of it to calm, peaceful, loving contentment. It emanates from you. You're a healer, Grace."

"Still. I think seeing and hearing things that aren't there is the very definition of insane." Grace smirked.

"Grace, just because you are the only one who can see or hear something doesn't mean it's not there. It only means that you're different. Lukkas said you can speak to him with your mind. If you are the only one who can hear him speak back, is he not there? Maybe it's true. Maybe you have someone out there looking for you and you're the only one who can hear them. Have you not ever considered that?"

"Then why can I only hear them in my dreams?"

"Would you prefer to hear them in the middle of the day?"

There was a knock at the door. A voice on the other side spoke. "Ladies, your train is boarding."

"Thank you, ma'am," Grace replied. "Time to go."

Galin was waiting for them outside of the lounge. "I thought I saw you two disappear in here. Everything as expected?"

"I'm not quite comfortable with the crowds yet," Viv answered.

"Where's Lukkas?" Grace asked.

"On the train with Vito. They're ensuring we have a private cabin. Viv, will you be fine with having Vito in the car?" Galin lowered his voice.

"You mean, do I want to drink my brother?" Viv whispered back.

"Yes."

"I'll be fine with him. It's the mob, the noise, and the motion I was overwhelmed with. I wasn't thirsty, just overloaded. I wanted to chase them. Is that strange?" She whispered back.

"No. We're natural predators. The urge will diminish soon." Galin offered her one arm and Grace the other.

"So, I shouldn't jump out the window and chase down some random horse's rider then?" Viv joked.

"Probably not this trip," Galin chided back.

"I would win," Viv said confidently.

"Naturally," Galin echoed her tone.

"If the two of you are finished, what car are we in?" Grace interrupted.

Galin led them forward. Lukkas was waiting for them at the door. He held out his hand to assist Grace up the steep stairs. Galin swept Viv off her feet to carry her into the car.

"Galin! Put me down this instant," she protested.

"Viv, the stairs are too steep for you to climb. You're injured. Remember?" Galin spoke softly into her ear.

"You could have warned me," Viv huffed.

"It was an impulse." Galin tilted his head forward, smirking. Viv reached up to remove his hat as he carried her through the door of their cabin. He placed her down gently on the tufted bench seat next to the window. Grace sat next to her with Lukkas by the door. Galin sat directly across from her, with Vito beside him. Even though Viv said she was fine, Galin wanted to ensure a buffer between them.

Galin and Lukkas engaged Vito in conversation regarding the daily operations of a winery. The brothers had both done their research, and they both planned to be involved in running the business. Neither, however, was planning to perform the day-to-day operational duties. Lukkas raised the question to Vito if he would be interested in assisting them with interviewing candidates for the vintner position. They were planning on offering Vito the position, but didn't want to look too desperate. Several candidates already had been scheduled to interview before the trip to Genova. They would wait and bring it up after they were unable to secure a qualified candidate. It would be better for Vito to think they were helping each other out. After all, it would be easier to justify Viv staying if Vito stayed on.

"You're not interested in running it yourselves?" Vito asked.

"It's not that we aren't interested. We have other businesses to attend to, as well as obligations to extended family," Galin explained. "I write business contracts and do all the sales and marketing for several ventures. Lukkas works with the money. He arranges financing, secures investments and loans, and keeps accounting for several other family members. His work ensures he travels fairly often. We both want to be as involved as possible, but it's impractical to think we can devote the necessary amount of time to this new venture. We realize we need someone we can count on to do things the right way without regular supervision. We need someone who can run the operations end of the business. We have four candidates to interview over the course of this week and we would appreciate it if you could weigh in. You have the experience to ask the questions we don't."

"I'd be happy to sit in. What type of candidate are you looking for?" Vito's interest was piqued.

Lukkas weighed in. "We want someone who understands the old ways of growing, but who also isn't afraid to incorporate new techniques if they will be of benefit. I've been reading about successes using a grafting technique to reduce parasite resistance. What are your thoughts on that?"

Vito nodded. "I've worked with a handful of growers at the warehouse who have been successful with grafting. They have told me the best results come from using a California stock of the same grape variety. It doesn't change the quality or consistency of the flavor either. I'd be interested in seeing that technique up close myself. Maybe start with a sample section so you can compare it to unaltered stock in the same field. I wouldn't do more than a few rows at the beginning."

Galin slapped Vito on the knee. "That's exactly what we're looking for. Someone who isn't afraid to try something new and at the same time is cautious enough not to bet the entire operation on it working. I knew you could come up with things we wouldn't be able to think of. I'm glad you'll be here this week, Vito."

The remaining four hours of the trip were spent in conversations about wine between the men. Grace and Viv had gotten bored with that topic early on. Grace began teaching Viv some common words and phrases in English. The language was fast becoming a standard for many parts of the world. Aside from Italian and French, which

Viv spoke fluently, she could muddle through with passable Spanish. Most vampires, by the hundred-year mark, were fluent in five or more languages. Viv was already in proper running to beat that average. Grace spoke eight current languages and a handful of dead ones. Language had evolved so much over the last millennium and a half; it took effort to merely keep up.

The last stop on the route was theirs. The station was nearly empty, as was the train. Less than a dozen passengers departed, aside from their group. At the top of the stairs, instead of arguing, Viv wrapped her arm around Galin's neck, allowing him to pick her up. He gracefully navigated the steep stairs with her in his arms. He stood waiting for the others to descend, still holding her. She tapped him on the chest with her free hand.

"I can walk to the carriage," she said loudly enough for everyone to hear.

"Oh, my apologies." Galin eased her to her feet. Vito appeared to dislike Galin's familiarity with his sister, although he held his tongue.

It was much cooler inland. The train had brought them into the foothills of an incredible mountain range. The air was sharp and crisp; a stark contrast to the damp salty air of the port city. The vineyard was close enough to allow for easy transportation, yet far enough that they were secluded. A small town had risen up around the train station. There was one main street comprising a boarding house, a proper bar, a tavern and a sizable general store, which also housed the post office and telegraph station. On the backside of the main street were a few skilled trade shops, a blacksmith, and stables.

The vineyard was a short ride from the train station. Vito kept looking up out of the carriage.

"What are those for?" He pointed to overhead cables suspended from timber poles.

"We have our own telephone. And we're having electricity installed. Brilliant times," Lukkas stated proudly. All types of technology excited him. He was always the first to embrace it, no matter what the cost.

"He's been obsessed with electricity since the Chicago World's Fair. Installing it out here has been painfully expensive, although I do see it as a sound investment. Personally, I'm more interested in the telephone. The potential for speaking to someone across the ocean, instead of waiting days to have a telegram returned or weeks for a letter, will revolutionize business," Galin added.

Grace laughed. "Men and their toys. We even have a motorcar. Women's needs are much simpler. I'm satisfied having indoor plumbing, and lighting that won't catch my dress on fire." She cocked her head at Lukkas. "You think of ways to go faster while we think of ways to make life easier."

"Why can't we do both?" Viv shrugged. "I am very interested in all this talk about flying machines."

"Of course you would be. You've always had your head in the clouds." Vito chuckled at her.

Viv was undeterred by her brother's teasing. "Someone needs to dream of these things. How else do you suspect we advanced from living in caves?"

Lukkas showed his support. "I agree, Viv. I'm very interested to see where all this flying business ends up."

"Not me. I'll keep my feet firmly on the ground." Vito crossed his arms. "It's not natural being in the clouds like that."

Viv bit her lip to keep from laughing. Galin lowered his head, watching her as he tried not to laugh himself. What wasn't natural was Vito riding through the countryside in a carriage with four immortals.

"You should keep your mind open to possibilities, Vito. People once thought it unnatural to cross the oceans. Now we send steam liners crossing every day with thousands of passengers." Lukkas opened his hands toward Vito.

"The difference is, when those engines stop working, people don't fall out of the sky. I don't see traveling like birds being something that is going to happen in my lifetime, anyway." Vito cocked his head sideways, peering up toward the sky.

"You might be surprised." Viv was having a difficult time holding back her laughter. Fortunately, Vito didn't turn to look at her. She certainly would have lost her composure if he had.

The carriage began passing low stone walls separating the road from the fields. They were old and crumbling in some places. Moss grew between the stones, flowing onto the ground in areas. The brothers had been investing in restoring the house to a livable condition, building new barrels and restoring the vines to a healthy state. The walls would have to wait until they started seeing a profit. Even then, though, they would likely only shore up the crumbling sections. They liked the feel the old, natural stone barrier gave approaching the villa.

It was a stark contrast to the new white stucco of the restored building's walls. It would take decades to match the deep, rich amber color of the original clay. Galin thought it sad when people tore out beautifully worked stone to replace it with new materials that didn't fit the landscape. He didn't think there was anything wrong with brick or cladding. He only thought it had to fit into the setting. Out here, the setting was old and rich, not sleek and modern. They had kept as much of the old work as they could. He only wished he had found it fifty years earlier, before it had deteriorated so badly.

As they approached the main house, only the stable hand was there to meet them. They didn't have any staff yet, aside from him and the driver. The construction crew was finished for the day and the cleaning woman came only twice a week while they were away. Since they didn't have a vintner, the fields had been empty since Galin had left. So much work needed to be done. Galin found it difficult to engage employees, as he was only learning the language. He desperately needed someone capable of setting the fields for winter. Once the work was complete, he would also need a house manager. It was his plan to have Viv take on those duties now that she had, in her own words, agreed to be his partner. It would be difficult to work her into being the lady of the house if Vito did not agree to come on as well. Galin needed to find a way to sell him on the idea that only he and Viv would work for the positions.

Everyone exited the carriage. The driver unloaded their baggage, allowing the stable hand to take the carriage to the barn. The driver was a younger Danish man they had brought to Italy with them. He wasn't particularly good at any one thing, but he was good to have around. His only downfall was that he was human. Galin would need to keep him away from Viv for the next three or four weeks, while she was most vulnerable to impulse.

"Sten, please take Vito's bags to the guest room. Viv will be staying with me." Grace spoke Danish to the driver.

"Yes, ma'am," he replied in kind, lifting the first of her four large trunks.

Grace told Viv she would be staying in her rooms.

"Grace, please, I couldn't put Lukkas out." Viv waved her hands at Sten.

"Lukkas has his own suite in his study. It's no bother at all. Besides," she whispered and leaned in close, wrapping her arm through Viv's. "I have the best bathtub."

Viv's eyes got huge as she gasped. She had never thought of having more than one private bath in a house.

"Come, let's get cleaned up. And then you can help me figure out something to feed them. I had a delivery brought in this morning. I have no idea what food is in the kitchen." Grace tugged on Viv's arm. "That, and I don't cook. So, I guess you'll be figuring out what to feed them." She giggled nervously.

"In that case, I get the bathtub first." Viv leaned into Grace as they headed into the house.

Galin turned to face Vito. "Well then, I guess we have a few hours to kill. Would you care for a tour?"

"I could use a good leg stretching. Lead the way," Vito replied.

"Lukkas, are you coming?" Galin looked to his side, eying Lukkas.

"Let me get the box secured and I'll catch up with you." Lukkas held up a large box of silver coin easily enough that Vito must have wondered if it was empty or filled with paper money.

Galin and Vito walked the grounds and the buildings. Both had as many questions as the other. It was clear, Galin really had very little idea how complex running a vineyard was.

"If I may be blunt, why did you buy a vineyard if you had no idea how to run one?" Vito smirked at Galin.

"Honestly, it was an investment opportunity I couldn't pass up. The man I purchased it from needed the money and you can never go wrong with purchasing land. There will never be more land on this planet, but there will always be more people. Land is always a sound option to own, if not for myself, then for my children and theirs later."

"Yes, but you have no idea what to do with it," Vito repeated.

"I am fortunate enough to have something many people in this area don't have: my brother and money. We can always find people who know what they're doing. We can also help a lot of people if we can get this back to a viable operation. If we can be successful, we can employ people who live here, so maybe they don't have to sell their own land and move their families somewhere else. I mean, yes, we are businessmen. We are here to make a profit. But if we can help the people who live here stay here, then everyone wins. Don't they?" Galin was heartfelt in bringing people up.

He did want to make a profit. Who wouldn't? But he also wanted to see this way of life continue. He had seen so many communities die off. So many of the old ways go by. So many societies disintegrate into nothing. He saw long-term potential here. In his view, a business like this could only grow. Land was gold. He truly hoped he was selling Vito on his vision. Even if Viv were completely out of the picture, he would still want Vito to run this place.

"I've seen a lot of loss in these places. I've also seen a lot of foreigners, people like you, come in and change things. Not respect the land or the culture. It's hard for me to see that happen again." Vito squinted as he looked over the land.

"Vito, I don't want to do that. I know enough to know I don't know anything. I'm looking for someone with the experience and ideas to make this work. I only want to make things better. I'm not looking to take away. I only want to add," Galin said humbly.

"Well, let's find you someone who can see things the way you want them to be." Vito said.

"No. Let's find someone who can see things the way they should be. Someone who respects the culture and isn't afraid to embrace new ideas that will allow it to flourish."

"Okay. Tell me about what you are willing to do for the right person. And what do you consider the right person?" Vito asked pertinent questions.

"I want someone who is willing to put themselves on the line for this to work. Lukkas and I aren't going to pay a salary. We want skin in the game. The right person needs to be willing to have a full third share. If this vineyard profits, they profit. If it fails, they do too. We will do whatever they tell us to do to make this work, but we need someone willing to go all in. Our problem lies in finding someone we can trust to put everything they have into it. Someone willing to live here. We can provide everything - all the necessities, as long as they are willing to put all they have into it," Galin explained.

"When you say you will provide the necessities, what do you consider necessities?" Galin hoped Vito had asked that question because he was interested, not simply for Galin's scheduled interviews.

Galin pointed back toward the villa. "Do you see the building over there? The house next to the sheep pen, across from the barn?" He hoped Vito could see it. Galin had no idea how bad human eyesight really was. To him, the building was enormous.

"Yes. I see it."

"That's the vintner's house. It has six rooms on two floors. That and its own kitchens behind it filled every week. No expenses for whomever takes our offer."

"And if they have children? What about education for them? Or do you expect them to work the vineyard?" All appropriate questions.

"If Lukkas and Grace don't have children of their own by then we would provide a tutor. There's no school in the town yet. And we still need to find someone to run the house so we could find a way to combine those, if possible." Galin wanted to throw that tidbit in there so he would think of Viv.

"By running the house, do you mean you need a housekeeper?"

"No, no. We already have someone to clean, and we are hoping to add to the house staff. We need someone who can do much more than that. I need a house manager. Someone organized to be in charge of the staff, the events we're hoping to hold here. Someone literate who can also assist me; who can be trusted to make sound decisions when I am away on business." Galin was hoping he had given a clear enough description of Viv's capabilities that Vito would see her as an option.

"What about Grace? Isn't she involved in the business already? She's the lady of the house, isn't she?" Vito made a valid point.

"Normally, I would say yes. Except Grace and Lukkas travel often. This is a full-time position she doesn't have the ability to fill. I also considered finding a couple that could fulfill both duties. Though I'm certain that's far too much to hope for."

"I think I understand exactly what you are hoping to find. Isn't that why you really brought me and Viv here in the first place?"

Galin was slightly shocked by Vito's bluntness, but not by his perception. He had all but propositioned the man. Vito was much smarter and more perceptive than Galin had given him credit for. He also felt Lukkas getting close to where they were and wanted to answer before he got to them.

"Yes," Galin nodded vigorously. "By the second evening we spent together, I thought you would be the perfect candidates for this venture. I didn't think I would come to like or respect you as much as I do, though. And I didn't think you would be at the bottling facility I toured. That was complete happenstance. My only regret is the horrible incident with Viv in the alley. I must believe after everything that happened; it must be fate that brought us together."

"What must be fate?" Lukkas asked as he came over the top of the hill.

"Me thinking this must be an opportunity I can't pass up. I only need to figure out a way to talk Viv into it," Vito answered, squinting as he bit the side of his lip.

"Well, that was anti-climactic. I thought you were going to let me make the offer." Lukkas seemed disappointed.

"Vito had already figured out our motive before I had even extended it. Which only reinforces my position that they are perfect for us." Galin splayed his hands toward Vito.

Lukkas extended his hand to Vito. "I would officially be honored to offer you the position. You and, of course, Viv, if she will accept."

Vito hesitated to take Lukkas's hand. "I think you should still interview candidates, at least for the short-term. I have another month's obligation to the bottling facility. We have a four-week contract starting on Wednesday that I have signed and must fulfill. That, and I still need to speak with Viv."

Lukkas took another step toward Vito. "You concern yourself with the contract. I will ensure Grace can talk Viv into the proposal. Deal?"

Relief washed over Vito's face. "Deal." He shook Lukkas's hand vigorously and then shook Galin's. "I should talk to her first to make her understand I am accepting the position. Then, if she has any trepidation, Grace can talk her into it. I'm certain she'll be better at it than I could be."

"Excellent." Galin was more relieved than Vito looked.

"She'll need to come back to the city with me for the month. I wouldn't want the perception of impropriety to stain her reputation. She's still young enough to find another husband if she doesn't appear tainted."

The words were acid to Galin's ears. The next month was the time she needed to stay close to them the most.

"Certainly. We would never want to soil her reputation," he answered, swallowing rancid fear.

"That and she needs to give proper notice to her employer," Vito added.

Lukkas shifted uneasily. He closed one eye and bit his lip. "Um. I think I actually ended her employment for her."

Vito and Galin looked at him, needing an explanation for his statement.

"How do you think you ended her employment?" Galin finally asked after an awkward amount of time.

"I went to see her employer before I went to tell Vito. I told him what had happened to Viv the evening before, and he was such a knob about it." Lukkas's tone became angry. "He didn't even ask after her condition. The only thing he wanted to know was how she was going to reimburse him for the night's profits and who was going to open the stand that morning! So, I threw the money pouch at him. He asked, 'Is this all?' He didn't even care that it had her dried blood on it! I told him he could go work the stand himself, and he slammed the door in my face."

Galin and Vito both shifted uncomfortably. Galin spoke, "Have you told her you quit for her yet?"

"No. I was hoping I wouldn't need to." Lukkas squirmed.

"How did you have her money pouch? And how did it have her blood on it?" Vito asked.

Lukkas had blurted out the events without thinking.

Lukkas looked him in the eyes. "She didn't want us to tell you. He stabbed her in the stomach in that alley. He took her money and left her to die. She is very injured and weak right now. The real question you should be asking is, who was the dead man in the alley the next morning without a hand?"

Vito had read the papers. Everyone had. They expected the man was the victim of a mob hit. Cutting off a hand was a sign of a thief. The death meant he had done something worse. He had never associated it with what had happened to Viv. He certainly would never have associated the incident with Lukkas or Galin.

Vito sucked air in through his teeth. He dropped to his knees, taking Lukkas's hand. He weakly exhaled the word "Mafioso." He sunk lower, his body shaking. "Thank you. A thousand times, thank you!" It was difficult for Galin to see this huge man groveling on his knees.

Galin grabbed Vito under his arm and brought him to his feet. He spun Vito hard to meet his eyes. He wasn't entrancing him. He only wanted to lock eyes with him.

"She doesn't know. She will never know. And you will never tell her you know the extent of her injuries. We protect our own. We see you - both of you - as our own. Do you understand?" Galin would prefer Vito see them as mafia as opposed to vampires, and he was willing to play the role to its conclusion.

"Yes. Yes, absolutely, yes. I owe you everything," Vito repeated.

Galin didn't like having the upper hand the way Vito had interpreted it. But he would take it and double down on the drama of the surreal scene.

"You need to fulfill your contract. To us, a man's word is everything." Galin grabbed Vito's shoulders with both hands. "You go back. When you're finished, you return to us. We're your family now."

Mission accomplished. Vito was grateful. He had accepted the position, which meant there was a great chance the winery would flourish. This also meant Galin had a basis for building a worldwide supply network. Viv would be able to stay without raising Vito's suspicions. It was a trust built on a technicality, but trust, nonetheless. Their 'mafioso' was a secret community of immortal creatures living amongst humans. Everything else was the truth. Now, he only needed to figure out a way to convince Vito to let Viv stay instead of taking her back to guard her reputation. If only it were the old days where he could just flippantly kill without remorse and take what he wanted. Okay, as a passing thought, that didn't even work. Galin had never been flippant about anything. And he certainly had never killed without remorse.

The hard part was over. He was confident he could figure this out. He needed to talk to Viv. Galin headed toward the house, leaving Lukkas and Vito on the ridge.

CHAPTER SEVEN

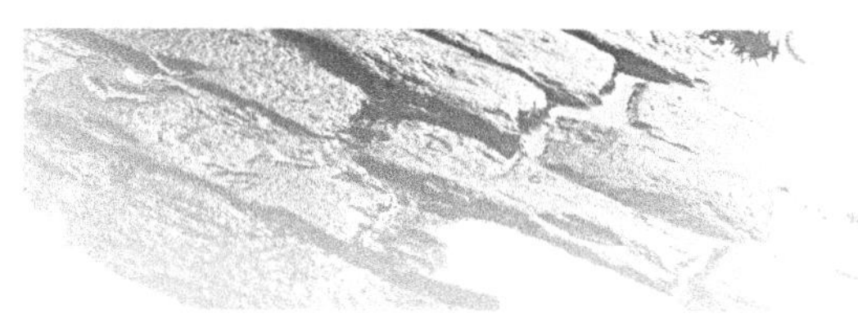

"I didn't ask you to save me, Galin." Viv had a serious look about her. She stood in the doorway of the study, her body stiff. The early morning sun stretched the full length of the room through the east facing window, landing on the hem of Viv's skirt.

"How could I not?" Galin slumped in his chair. He wouldn't apologize for saving her. It did sadden him that he had changed her into something others viewed as a monster. Every hour he struggled with the guilt.

"As much as I ache to be close to you, all of you, I can't stay here. You need to let me go back. It's only a month." She looked so sad to him.

"Viv, if people find out what you are, they'll kill you. I couldn't live with that. Not after what I forced you to become. It's my fault." Galin rubbed his fingers through his hair. His heart ached. It was distressing to think she would be in the city by herself. Yes, Vito would be with her, but he didn't know what she was. Vito wouldn't be able to help her get through the next few weeks. He wouldn't be able to help calm her urge to feed. She wouldn't have anyone safe to feed from if it became necessary. Terrible situations raced through his head all at once, overlapping the worst thoughts atop of each other.

"You don't have a choice. This must look right. Vito would never let me stay with a man I've only known a week. And he can't know what I am now. I know you understand this, Galin. As much as you loathe it, you know it has to be my choice." Her body stiffened even further, if that was possible.

He sighed, sinking deeper into his chair. "I know."

He rubbed his forehead and took a drink of wine. "It's one thing to disappear completely. It's far more difficult to stay and maintain a level of morality in such a socially narrow society." He gulped down the rest of his glass and put it down hard on the table. "I'm afraid for you being alone down there, Viv."

"What choice do we have, Galin? I'm not an idiot. I realize it will be difficult. You need to help me. You need to make sure I understand what I'll be facing. All of what I'll be facing. Not just the easiest parts you've been telling me up to now." She stepped into the room, closing the door behind her.

"You haven't needed to know the worst parts because you're here with us."

Viv placed her hand on her hip and rolled her eyes. "Did you mean to reinforce my exact point, Galin? I'm not going to be here for the next month. You… you understood the argument, didn't you?" If she had wanted to make him feel stupid, she succeeded.

Her body lost some of the tension when she crossed the room to the bar. She poured herself a glass out of the bottle Galin had opened. As he walked up behind her, he could feel her panic. She did a good job outwardly covering her emotions, but it didn't work when he was close to her. He reached around her, taking the glass from her hand, setting it on the bar. Their bodies were almost touching. He felt the warmth emanating from her back onto his chest. He placed his hands on the bar on either side of her. She didn't turn around. He didn't touch her.

They stood motionless, feeling each other without physical contact. He breathed in her scent of lavender, exhaling lightly on the back of her neck. She released her rigid form, leaning back lightly against his chest. She reached down, taking his hands and guided his arms to cross around her waist. He felt her body trembling. When he looked in the window, he saw her reflection watching him, as tears silently streamed down her face. His heart shattered for her. Why had he done this to her? How could he let her leave the vineyard alone? He would do anything if she would only stay. He didn't care how it looked. His thoughts were empty. The only thing that existed in the world at that moment was Viv.

The unexpected motion of her spin away from him sent him reeling backward.

"I can't believe it's so simple." Viv spun around wide-eyed, grabbing the sides of Galin's face.

Galin took hold of her wrists, clasping her hands into his chest. "Viv, what are you talking about? What's so simple?"

She grabbed his shirt. "Don't you see? We can turn him."

Galin's heart sunk at her words. It was anything but simple. He wasn't even supposed to have turned her.

"Viv, you don't know what you're asking. I can't." Galin hadn't told her the extent of the possible punishment. She had no idea how close she had come to losing her life when he turned her without permission. This time, there wouldn't be any mitigation. The Board would execute Vito if they turned him.

"I know exactly what I'm asking. You owe me a life." The anger seethed out of her.

"I gave you a life!" He raised his voice to match hers and backed away.

"Not one I asked for!" she yelled even louder, flying up on him. "I'll do it myself if you won't. But if I have to, you'll never see either of us again," she spat through gritted teeth.

In an explosion of rage, she shoved him harder than she knew she could. He flew back through the air, slamming into the wall. It shook the entire villa. Cracked plaster fell to the floor around him. Dust particles hung like smoke in the air. It rattled him. The painful truth in her words weighed harder than any physical violence. He had suspected from the beginning she was on the precipice of an eruption. The further down she pushed her emotions, the more explosive it would become. He was glad it had happened here, with him.

When he looked up, he saw the terror in her eyes. She stood still as stone as the realization of what she had done washed over her. This was exactly what he was most afraid of for her. The resentment she felt for him. The uncontrollable emotional rage that came early in the turn due to the violent nature of her death. If she had shoved Vito like that, she would have killed him. There would be no way she could live with herself if that happened. He approached her slowly, taking her hand. She began shaking as they slid down to the floor. Her eyes were closed as she leaned her forehead against his chest. He pressed his chin into her hair. As her sire, Galin was the only one, aside from Grace, who could calm her.

"Galin. I can't go back to the city with him, can I?" Viv whispered. The realization of what he had been telling her set in. "What are we supposed to do?"

Galin gently lifted her chin, tilting his head down to meet her eyes. He whispered back to her. "We tell him why you can't leave. If he wants the turn, it must be his choice. It has to be done by our laws."

"Galin, we can't tell him. It's too soon. He won't understand." Viv was clouded by her emotions. She wasn't thinking there were any other options.

"If he reacts badly to the information, we can entrance him into forgetting we told him."

"Then why can't we entrance him into letting me stay?" Viv grabbed the front of his shirt.

"I'm not certain I can make a suggestion like that. Making someone forget is easy, especially if it's something they don't want to remember in the first place. Suggesting an entirely new thought is complicated." Galin placed his hands on her arms.

The study door slammed open, banging hard into the wall. The sound jolted them. Vito did not appear to appreciate the position Galin had Viv in on the floor. He stomped across to the couple, snatching Viv up by the wrist. He glared at Galin.

"What did you do to her?"

Viv answered before Galin could. "Nothing. He didn't do anything to me."

"Then why are you crying? You don't cry for nothing. You don't cry at all." Vito seemed as confused as he was angry.

Lukkas appeared in the doorway to see Vito holding Viv's wrist hard. It was apparent she had been crying. And Galin was leaning back on the floor. Galin sprung to his feet.

"What's going on in here?" Lukkas asked in a restrained tone.

"Your brother did something to her, and she's defending him," Vito stated more calmly than Galin had expected.

Vito's eyes were still on Viv. When he turned to address Lukkas, he saw the large indentation and broken plaster near the door.

"What the hell? You threw her into the wall?!" Vito turned on Galin, still holding Viv's wrist, dragging her with him.

"No Vito! Stop!" Viv yelled at him.

Vito took two more steps forward. Viv grabbed his arm with her free hand. She ripped her wrist out of his grasp and pulled him backward. He lost his balance, stumbling a few steps sideways. He would have fallen if Viv hadn't righted him, holding most of his weight. He pulled back, baffled at how she could have lifted him in her supposedly injured and weakened state.

"He didn't throw me into the wall." She peered at him cautiously, tilting her head. "I threw him into the wall."

"Don't lie to me, Vivienne!" he sneered at her. Vito either didn't want to believe her or couldn't believe her.

Galin nodded at his brother, signaling him to be ready. Lukkas swallowed, preparing to block Vito from charging the door. Lukkas pegged him for the storming off type. Even though Vito was only human, he was big, and had solid muscle. He could still give the far slenderer Lukkas a hit he would feel.

At that moment, Grace entered the room. She heard the commotion. Thinking quickly, she devised a different explanation.

"Galin, I told you that you shouldn't be teaching her inside."

Galin wasn't exactly sure where she was going with this yet. "I didn't think it would be an issue."

Viv and Lukkas looked at her, trying not to reveal their confusion. Vito appeared befuddled and still angry.

Grace continued feigning irritation. "Self-defense is a messy affair. You could break things. Viv, why are you so upset?"

The light bulb appeared to come on for Grace's three co-conspirators.

Viv answered, "I thought I had hurt Galin when he hit the wall. The plaster broke away so easily and he fell to the floor."

"This old place will fall apart if you even touch the wall. See?" Grace pressed her hand against the wall beside her, crumbling some of the plaster. "Now, take this business outside, please."

Vito's face washed red, this time with embarrassment instead of anger. "You were teaching her to defend herself?"

Galin smoothed his shirt. "After the incident in the city, I felt it my duty to make sure she could do so if necessary. I also feel it prudent she does not travel alone."

"I have to agree with you on that. The city isn't the safest place for a woman alone. I apologize for my suspicion." Vito gazed at the floor, wringing his hands. This was all so confusing to him. These people he had befriended so easily behaved strangely. What he thought they were could partially account for it, but now Viv was acting strangely too.

"I would have likely made the same mistake given our apparently compromising position on the floor." Galin didn't enjoy lying to Vito. It wasn't the right time to tell him what they were. It would be easier when he returned, after he had lived amongst them for a while.

Grace had also come up with a solution to the predicament Viv was in. "Since we're all here, I wanted to let you know I will be traveling to France tomorrow for the birth of my cousin's first child. I would appreciate a travel companion if you would like to come with me, Viv."

"Oh Grace, I would love to. I was not looking forward to going back to the city after that traumatizing attack. You don't mind me traveling with Grace, do you, Vito? At least then you won't need to worry about the perception of my being alone here with Galin and Lukkas." Viv had intentionally made it a request he would look like an ass to refuse after the discussion of not letting women travel alone. It was apparent Viv was grateful for Grace's intervention.

"Well, um, no. I mean, I thought you wanted to go home. I have my contract to finish." Vito rubbed his head. He didn't seem to want to let her stay behind, but she had put him in a position where he couldn't refuse her.

Viv set a sad expression, looking up at him with her huge dark eyes. "I prefer not to go back yet, if it's all the same. You can pass along my sentiments, can't you? I think everyone will understand if I prefer to be away for a time."

Galin realized Viv didn't enjoy playing a meek role. It was advantageous for her to play it well this time. She needed time away from her brother, away from humans altogether, if possible. He thought the exposure to another clan would give her a better understanding of the community, too. Being with Grace was the safest place for her.

"How long will you be gone?" Vito asked Grace.

"About six weeks. It's a brief trip." Grace smiled, taking Viv's arm. It would take far longer to blood nurse a pure born. Grace thought six weeks would sound like a more acceptable length of time to Vito.

Vito's expression softened at seeing Viv and Grace's excitement. "How could I possibly say no? You deserve a bit of happiness."

Viv held her breath when he leaned down to kiss her on the forehead.

"You two take care of each other."

"We will!" Viv exclaimed, exhaling.

Grace pulled her toward the door. "We have so much to pack."

Lukkas rolled his eyes as they passed him. He didn't think Grace had even had time to unpack yet.

There were so many changes coming for all of them. Grace and Viv left on the train the next morning. Vito left a few days later as scheduled. When he returned to the vineyard within a few weeks, after completing his contract, the three men busied themselves hiring workers and preparing the fields for winter. They had a lifetime of work ahead of them.

There had been so much work, they hadn't minded when Grace and Viv stretched their visit to nearly four months in the French countryside. Grace taught Viv English and Dutch while she served her duties as blood nurse to Addie's great-granddaughter. While there, Addie took Viv on excursions to London and Amsterdam. She met several members of other clans. She learned their ways and detailed their histories. Viv was well liked and well respected. The community deemed her a welcome addition.

Shortly after she and Grace returned to Italy, Viv, and Galin planned to have a very small hand-fasting ceremony at the vineyard. Making plans was the simple part. Galin wasn't looking forward to what he had to face before it could happen.

CHAPTER EIGHT

"**W**hy would you want to marry my sister? You barely know each other. You should find a young wife. Don't you want someone who can give you children?" Vito asked, throwing his hands up and shaking his head.

Galin chuckled. "Vivienne is not as old as you seem to think she is."

"She's not as young as *you* seem to think she is. She's thirty-seven!" Vito retorted.

"Vito! Don't you know anything about women? You can't tell someone a woman's age," Galin smirked. He felt relieved the conversation was going in a better direction than he had expected.

Now it was Vito's turn to belt out a hearty laugh. "Are you sure you won't regret it in a few years? I mean, she's not the easiest woman to live with. She's controlling and opinionated. She'll never be what you would consider a traditional wife."

The months alone with Galin and Lukkas had their desired impact. It had softened Vito's opinion of the men. Time had also raised his suspicion they weren't what he believed that first day he had come to the vineyard. They were something unexplainable, but undoubtedly not mafioso.

"I'm not what most women would consider a traditional husband. Do you not want me to marry your sister?" Galin asked.

"I want my sister to be happy."

"I want her to be happy, too," Galin said.

Vito rubbed his neck and shifted in his seat. The fingers of his free hand drummed against the armrest of his chair in a slow, thoughtful rhythm. Galin and his brother had brought him and his sister opportunities they couldn't imagine were possible. He had seen firsthand what they were doing for the townspeople, but he was struggling with the things he had seen when they thought he wasn't looking. The strength and speed of these men were unnatural. Even Vivienne's own display months ago was unexplainable. The conundrum of those instances set against this man sitting in front of him, patiently waiting for Vito's blessing, created a tug-of-war in him. Did he ask? Or did he accept what he had been given without question?

Vivienne could no longer take the silence on the other side of the door. She burst in, disrupting Vito's muddled contemplation.

"Say yes, Vito."

He lifted his eyes to meet hers as she stood confidently over him. Whatever was going on with these people, Viv was evidently aware of it. There was no hesitation in her words or her stance.

Setting his suspicions aside, Vito gave his blessing.

A few weeks later, Vivienne and Galin wed under an arbor of the vines that would determine their future. The only attendees outside of Grace, Lukkas, and Vito were Ivan and Addy, whom Viv had grown close to.

Viv never did get to have a turning ceremony, and she didn't get a large wedding with grandeur and frills, but what she got was a new life.

Vito saw how content she was, how free and unburdened she felt, and how much she loved Galin.

She had learned both Danish and English within their first year. Running the household was something she excelled at. No detail ever went unattended while she was in charge. She excelled at charming any guest or client who walked through the door, ensuring none left with a negative experience.

Vito eventually learned what she had become when Vivienne became pregnant. The gestational period for a vampire lasted only one hundred days. It was something that couldn't be hidden or explained away. After his initial alarm at the revelation, Vito came to accept what they were. It had taken little convincing for him to request to join his beloved sister in immortality. He was accepted by the Board, taking the turn himself a year after Viv and Galin's first daughter, Violet was born.

Vivienne would go on to find her purpose in the dark days of Mussolini's dictatorship. She was the first woman to join the opposition in their region, once the formerly beloved leader's xenophobic intentions had become clear. Much to Galin's chagrin, she flourished in her rebellious role. Her high-level acumen for planning helped create a local network, which aided those attempting to escape the black shirt squads sent to silence them. Her efforts protected thousands from extermination or imprisonment. Galin was proud of her and supported her in theory, but was worried about her becoming involved in human political affairs.

The only real fight they ever had was when Galin forced the family to move to Switzerland before World War II. They had overstayed their time and were becoming noticed after nearly forty years in the same location. Vivienne cried as they left, upset at abandoning her undertaking to others more vulnerable than herself, thinking it was possibly the only regret she would have in her life.

Their fledgeling business stumbled during the American prohibition and two world wars, but afterward, their lives flourished. In the next decades, the family would go on to have wineries all over the world. The network they created would be used to free all vampires from the curse of consuming blood. The community would flourish in the technological age. They would evolve and dominate their chosen paths as immortals on a mortal world. They couldn't yet imagine the events that would come leading to their entire existence being changed forever. It would be an existence free from the restrictions of a single planet or even a single dimension. They would embrace their destiny as immortals in The Everything.

ALSO BY

JOYCE SERRANO

THE TURNED GODS SERIES

Original Grace - Book 1
Immortals in the Everything - Book 2

THE TURNED GODS - CHARACTER COMPANION SERIES

Galin's Alley
Lilly's Game

www.ingramcontent.com/pod-product-compliance
Lightning Source LLC
Chambersburg PA
CBHW061221210726
48294CB00006B/1932